ROOTS DOWN TO HELL

MATTHEW LOUIS

ROOTS DOWN TO HELL

gutterbooks.com

Roots Down to Hell

ISBN: 978-1-939751-29-4

Visit www.gutterbooks.com.

Printed in the USA

"It is the same with man as with the tree . . . The more he seeketh to rise into the height and light, the more vigorously do his roots struggle earthward, downward, into the dark and deep—into the evil."

—Friedrich Nietzsche,
Thus Spoke Zarathustra

ROOTS DOWN TO HELL

1

Sometimes, whatever you think you have, whatever you think you are, just ends. You step onto a quiet street, confident about how your day, or the next year, or the rest of your life, is going to play out, and only when it's much too late do you realize that you didn't check for oncoming traffic. Only when you're a broken, flattened thing, trying to pull oxygen into your crushed lungs, do you realize what an unutterable fool you are, and what a fool you've always been.

That is something like what went through my head on that April afternoon when the spring break at my wife's college began. I found myself, with hardly a memory of how I'd gotten there, standing in the kitchen of the little house Michelle and I lived in, looking down at Michelle's unmoving form, my grandmother's maple rolling pin dangling from my right hand.

In my defense, I had a stab wound on my left shoulder from which an astonishing amount of blood was dribbling, a red stream snaking down my inner arm, a scarlet stain growing on my white T-shirt. I was breathing in convulsive gulps and periodic spasms of subsiding rage squirmed through my body. I could hardly keep my knees from buckling as I shuffled over and clacked the rolling pin onto the formica, then slumped over the counter, waiting for my system to stabilize.

In spite of myself, I peered over my shoulder. I muttered, half-sobbing, "Come on, Michelle, *move*." My wife was on her stomach with her upper half across the entryway from the kitchen to the living room. She wore a tight, black, girl-cut T-shirt that was slightly ridiculous on her hefty frame. Her backside, pointed half toward me in her factory-faded jeans, looked gargantuan, her poor cell phone pinioned in a back pocket. Her head, adorned in her confusion of dark brown hair, was turned away from me. I could see no signs of damage. The steak knife was lying next to her limp hand, on the living-room side of the threshold. A smear of blood—barely a dab, really—was evident on the point of the serrated blade.

I told myself that this was all her fault, tried to get my ire up, but it wouldn't take. The only idea that had any meaning was that I was fucked. Thoroughly and for all time.

But then there was something, a fleeting thought, a glimmer of desperation trying to become defiance. I swiveled my eyes down, felt the burrowing pain in my shoulder, gawked at the growing, bright red stain on my shirt. My heart was slamming away like a machine with a stuck throttle, making it difficult to catch my breath, pushing the life-fluid steadily out of the hole Michelle had made in me. I imagined myself losing so much blood that I collapsed, and then the two of us being found here, and Michelle really being . . . gone . . . and the cops seeing exactly what had happened, shaking their heads, instantly establishing my guilt beyond any reasonable doubt.

I set my teeth, straightened and turned so my ass was on the counter-edge. I stretched my sleeve up with my right hand and heard myself hiss, "*Jesus!*" as I noted the size of the opening and the way the blood just kept puking out of it. I reached past the sink, caught hold of the dank-smelling dishrag tossed there, balled the cloth up, and pushed it under the sleeve. I pressed as hard as I could manage, sucking air through my teeth and blinking at tears.

After a minute or two, with the world in a constant, gentle spin, the bleeding seemed to have slowed, maybe even stopped, although the dishrag felt as if it was already soaked through. I blinked vigorously, made my eyes focus, and glared at Michelle. I willed her to twitch, seeing in my mind's eye how she was going to jerk awake and start lifting herself up—but with my actual eyes only seeing her lying there, second after second after second, as still as a photograph.

And then the spots floating at the edge of my vision began multiplying upon themselves, overtaking reality, until there was nothing else, and I felt myself going over, tumbling into nothing, and never landing. The last thought I had—a thing which felt momentous to me—was: *If it hadn't been for the fucking cat . . .*

*

The fucking cat. It had nothing to do with anything, really, but it was why I didn't just let Michelle walk out of my life. When I came in the front door after work, squinting in the diminished light, I was confronted by the sight of my wife emerging from the hallway with her baby-blue backpack slung over one shoulder and her cat under her arm. It was the fact of her carrying the cat that began setting off alarms. That, and the guilty horror that stole through her eyes as our gazes locked.

I pushed the door shut behind me, not quite panicked yet. "What are you doing?" I said. "Are you going somewhere?"

"Kevin," she said, momentarily paralyzed, stupefied. "I'm sorry. I left you a note."

"You *what?* Where are you going?"

The cat peered at me with its placid contempt. Michelle had named it Roxy for no particular reason. It had a black face with a white streak on its chin, like paint flung off a brush. Michelle repeated, "I'm sorry," and moved toward the kitchen entry, which led to the back door, which led to the carport, where she would get in her car and leave.

I found myself thinking of the time Michelle and I watched the old, black-and-white *Invasion of the Body Snatchers*, where the hero hears exactly the voices he knows, sees exactly the same faces, but the minds behind those voices and faces have become the property of some other entity. The comfy old friends and neighbors, and even wives, have become agents of the alien agenda.

My wife, I thought, had been body-snatched.

It was evident in how she dressed, too. Today, as I gaped

at her, Michelle looked about as good—about as sexy, anyway—as I had ever seen her look. That might not be saying much, because Michelle was not only about thirty pounds overweight, she had something of a piggy look about her. Her nose angled up in an unusual way, as if held in place by an invisible finger, and she was only about five feet tall, which isn't a bad thing for a woman, but the overall effect, if one was being a little too honest, was rather strikingly that of a pig-human hybrid. Back in the good days, when she was somebody else, when I was glad just to have a real, live girl to touch and she drew confidence from my enthusiasm, she'd told me that the boys in school actually used to call her Miss Piggy. It had become such a problem, she confessed, that her parents had finally taken her out of public school and placed her in Riverbend Academy, which cost so much that the administrators couldn't allow any of their charges to be tortured too overtly. All I had ever told her, from the first time the topic came up, was that she was just perfect as far as I was concerned. And the thing is, until recently—until today—that was the truth.

But her newfound sexiness was something else again, and I guess it's why I never saw what was coming. I knew that Michelle had become good friends with a lesbian schoolmate named Sabrina, but what did I know about lesbian relationships? How was I to know that one woman plays the man and the other remains a woman—and then some? Michelle had begun putting her attributes on display the last couple of months, wearing clothes that exaggerated her shape, pushed her extra weight into the right places like she was some kind of balloon animal.

I saw it now—saw the whole thing—and I knew she was already gone, but I couldn't accept it. I moved, not too aggressively, almost apologetically, to block her path. My hands were raised. "You have to tell me what's going on!" I said. "Michelle! Hey! Look at me!"

"Kevin, just don't."

But I just did. I said, "No, no, no. Whatever you're thinking, Michelle—no. It's not going to happen." And that was how it started. We ended up, for a few awful minutes, in a standoff in front of the entryway to the kitchen, me pitching pleas and demands and her batting them away. The cat's expression began to betray annoyance.

When Michelle finally told me there was someone else, I blacked out for an instant, like a boxer who has caught a perfect jaw-shot. But I recovered, slugged my way out of it, smirked and called her a sneaky whore. I told her that college boys were spoiled shitheads like her, and she was going to learn—oh, she was going to learn. She was doomed, I sneered. Nobody was going to stick by her like I would have. She was barely a five, more like a three; she couldn't pick and choose. Didn't she know that she looked—quite literally, I said; not even joking—like a fucking pig?

That statement seemed to leave the air around us smarting. I had never played that card before. I could see her body tense as the words found their mark. Her face pushed forward and her mud-colored eyes jerked back and forth, taking in both my eyes.

She readjusted her grip on Roxy, shrugged her backpack strap up, and said, "It's not a college boy, you stupid fool. I'm going to be with Sabrina."

"You . . ." I said. I could not make the thing go down.

Michelle was nodding, a mirthless smile warping her face, and she said, "Now you know. From one fucking pig to another." And she breezed into the kitchen.

Now, out of options, I took hold of her backpack handle and hauled her backward, causing her to stumble over her heels until the counter stopped her. The cat squirmed more deliberately and Michelle let it slither free, gain the floor, and pad out of the kitchen. I positioned myself between Michelle and any escape route—cornered her in the kitchen—explaining simply, stupidly, that I couldn't allow this. I saw her unbridling her indignation, eyes widening, teeth showing. "Did you just put your hands on me?" she said, her voice thickened.

"It was the backpack, Michelle. I pulled your backpack. I didn't put my hands on you." My voice was too calm to be mine. My lungs would not quite fill. This wasn't really happening.

She glanced where the cat had gone, as if that had significance. Her lips worked, made strange shapes that she finally gave form to. "You're a racist!" she spat. "You're homophobic scum! I know your whole story, Kevin!"

This, I knew, was the heart and soul of what was happening. It was that college that had body-snatched my wife, made her a fanatical enemy of my whiteness and my maleness, drove her into Sabrina's short, plump, tattooed arms. This year, Michelle had switched her major from English Lit—the thing that had originally brought us together—to Human Services, whatever the fuck that is. We had debated social justice topics until we were both sick of our lines, and the more we argued, the more exasperated she became, and the more smug and dismissive I became.

But that's how they get you. You think it's too ridiculous to bother with. You think it can't possibly have staying power. But while you're laughing it off, the bodies are being snatched.

"Spare me the buzzwords, Michelle," I now said. "I already know the commie faggots have taken over your little piggy brain."

I felt a thrill as the words left my mouth. I was going for shock and awe, trying to reset the power dynamic. In the past, just a hint of disdain could reduce her to tears, put me back in the driver's seat. But I felt my own resolve begin to crumble as I saw the change in her expression.

It was like she was downshifting, preparing for a climb up a slippery grade. Eyes dancing, she said, "You know what, Kevin? Remember a couple months ago? When I stayed with Sabrina for a few days? You know what that was?"

I blinked at her. I couldn't make myself see this person, this personality, as the girl who had wanted to marry me. I thought she was going to tell me about her first time having lesbian sex, as if I hadn't already guessed—

"I was pregnant," she said. "I was going to have a baby, your baby, and it was probably going to be a boy."

Only now did I feel my baffled frustration drawing to a laser point, becoming hate to match her hate. I knew she told the truth. Her new birth-control pills had made her constantly sick, so we had switched to condoms for the last year, but we generally ended up taking our chances with the pull-out method, of which I had never mastered the timing.

She knew exactly what she was doing. In the good days, a year ago, we had agreed that we were going to start a family, and toyed with the idea of her quitting school to be a stay-at-home mom. We had talked, as couples do, about what our children would look like and how many we ought to have. I had told her how being a father, and especially having a son, was like an impossible dream for me. I had even gotten choked up, confessing that I wanted to make up for the failures of my own father.

"You were pregnant," I said, my voice strangling. "And?"

"And I had an abortion, Kevin. I killed it, I killed your baby, and it felt *good.* I freed myself from *this* fucking bullshit." A mist of spittle left her mouth as she spoke the last words, and she waved her hand in a gesture that took in my whole being. White trash, white male, ignorant, evil . . .

I surged toward her, knowing very well that I should not do this. I saw the moisture on her forehead now, shining in the late afternoon light that pressed through the kitchen window. Her bushy dark hair was like an expressionist painting. Her brown eyes seemed to bulge, the pupils shrunken to dots with the threads of yellow around them more apparent than ever. She looked up at me, not breathing, wavering between satisfaction and fear, uncertain whether she had broken me. She didn't believe I was going to hit her, even as I knotted my hand into a fist and brought it level with my shoulder. She thought it was a silly gesture, a macho act, and she sneered and said, "What—" as I let go. All the anger seemed to flow into that arm, my body twisted with the swing, and her face crumpled, eyes mashing shut, as her teeth ground under my knuckles.

She stepped back, clutching her face, making animal noises, saying, "*Oh my god! Oh my god!*" into her hands. The backpack slid down and hung at the crook of her arm. Now she went into Victim of Domestic Abuse mode, lowering her hands so I could see the blood on her mouth, her eyes softened by shock. The backpack dropped to the floor.

She held her palms toward me. "Kevin!" she said, "Please stop. Just let me go, okay?" It was as if I had a gun trained on her. Or maybe she knew what she deserved. Or maybe there really was something disturbing in my eyes. I hardly knew I was looming toward her, and I was saying something about the abortion, and lesbians, and spoiled cunts, and asking her if she thought she was going to get away with this. I probably did sound, and look, a little crazy. She had gotten what she wanted. I was broken.

Her expression suddenly changed as I got close enough to touch her. Her gaze flared across the countertop, and her hand flashed over. I had cut up an apple with a steak knife that morning, left the knife on the counter in the sticky apple juice like the entitled man-child I was, and now the knife was in her fist, passed just like that from left hand to right, waving in front of my face. "You better back the fuck off!" she said, and this is where it got stupid, because my eyes flashed over, and there was Grandma's rolling pin, still where Grandpa had mounted it three decades before, in its cheese-ball countrified holder on the wall, and no sooner had I seen it then it was in my hand.

The notion I had was to just keep the knife blade away from me. Weapon against weapon. But I did have her cornered, and maybe she panicked—or maybe she was swept up in righteous, antiracist-queer-feministic anger—and she did some kind of fencing thrust, got the point of the blade so far into my shoulder that it must have hit bone.

I sucked breath like a comic actor, eyes bugging at the small tear in my shirt, which was already dark red. The helpless horror was utterly humiliating, and then utterly enraging. The force behind that knife-thrust was so spectacularly uncalled-for. I would have to go get stitched up now, and after she got away she would call the police and send me to jail too, since I struck first. She and Sabrina would be thrilling about this situation, about how I had confirmed all the stereotypes and got what I deserved, until they were withering away together in an assisted living facility. All of that was in my mind, maybe not clearly articulated, but understood, as Michelle hustled past me with, I swear, a look of elation on her face.

So as she passed, when she thought she was home-free, when she was at exactly the right distance, I gave it to her with the rolling pin, just behind her right ear. That didn't do it, but it sent her crashing into the wall.

What I did next, asking her through clenched teeth if she regretted killing my baby *now*, did it.

2

And then, as I stood there dripping blood, my heart trying to punch its way out of my chest and the world swinging queasily beneath my feet, the curtain was drawn across my consciousness. I went over like a falling tree, tumbled into the great black void, thinking as I fell about that goddamned cat.

I was probably only out for a few seconds, however, before the sound of anguished crying drew me back to reality.

Roxy was the noisiest cat I had ever encountered or even heard of. Its common greeting to its humans was the sort of cat-yell you might expect if its back half was caught in a trap. We had deduced that this had to do with it being taken from its mother too soon and fed from a eye-dropper by the people who had given it away on Facebook marketplace. It now thought of all humans as large mother cats that it was obliged to shamelessly demand nourishment from. When my eyes opened I had the bizarre experience of being on the same level with the animal, peering numbly at its glossy black body, white on the underside, with two white feet. Above me was a full burst of late afternoon sunlight, swimming with dust particles as it streamed in the window over the sink, and the mewing cat, and the whole world, looked to me like an overexposed photograph. I moved only my eyes. The clock on the oven said "6:02." The cat stood next to Michelle, tail twitching, calling out to her to feed it. I rolled and began to raise myself and when Roxy realized that I was awake, she turned her eerily intense, liquid eyes to me and stepped in my direction, wailing.

The cat's cries intensified as I pushed on the floor, then pulled on the counter, and finally got my feet under me. I felt the world pitching and rolling, then I felt the helpless tipping and almost went down again, but I slouched against the counter until it passed. I sensed the blood starting to trickle steadily from my shoulder as my heart continued its relentless thudding and my blood pressure increased. The dark, shiny left side of my shirt glinted distractingly in the bottom of my vision. There were gaudy red smears, interspersed with big, comical globules of blood, on the linoleum. The linoleum was an outdated brown, and as the edges of the smears dried, they seemed to become part of the flooring. I wondered what the hell the cat must make of this scene.

I walked stiff-legged across the kitchen and snatched the cat-food bag from the shelf by the back door, discovering as I lifted it that it was nearly empty. When I looked down,

Roxy's stainless steel dish was gone. I felt a familiar prickling of spite for Michelle's ruthless, feminine efficiency. Nothing overlooked. She had packed the cat's dish, but noted what was left in the bag and decided to leave it. I opened the bag's ziplock seal and upended it, creating a small pile of kibbles where the bowl should have been, then letting the bag fall to the floor. The cat's yelling stopped as it pushed its face into the food.

My shoulder was leaking the whole time. I had to do something about it. I only had so much blood in me. I made it over Michelle without looking at her directly, and zombie-walked across the living room, down the hall, and into the bathroom. When I hit the switch the guy in the mirror was an actor made up for a horror movie. Frazzled hair. Chalk complexion. Fried-egg eyes. Blood smeared every which way. I got the T-shirt off one way or another, dragging at it, bending myself in half, my left arm almost no help. Facing the mirror again, I examined the wound. It ran vertically, its little sideways mouth half an inch long, expelling life-fluid in a casual way, like a faucet given a quarter turn. I cursed Michelle and jerked the hand towel from its rack. I cranked the water on, wet the towel, got the obvious blood off my face and torso, and mashed the towel over the wound, letting my face contort at the vicious stinging. I zombie-walked through the house again, shirtless. I glanced as I opened the front door. Michelle's head was turned so I couldn't avoid the pale mask of her face. Her eyes, thankfully, were closed.

I had an objective. There was a roll of duct tape tossed on the passenger's-side floor of my truck. This property was the sectioned-off corner of an old farm. What we called the driveway was just a big, graveled space. The road we lived on was a few hundred feet over, and a car passed every minute or so. Anyone driving by might glance, but nobody would take any special interest in a shirtless guy walking to his truck. I tried to make my knees bend right, to walk normally, to look like there was nothing unusual about the towel held to my shoulder.

Back inside, I pressed the door shut with my elbow, stumbled through the now-surreal house, to the bathroom, and didn't even look at the kitchen entrance as I passed. I retrieved the washcloth that was dried stiff in the bath stall, and folded it over the wound. I managed to get the duct tape started, got a layer of it over the washcloth, cinched it tight, then got another layer, and another, over it, crossing the tape at different angles. The skin pinched obnoxiously if I moved the arm too much, and my fingers tingled from the restricted circulation, but the bleeding would stop.

I went to the bedroom. The blinds were open, the last daylight sifting in through the poplar that towered outside the window. I stood and stared. The closet was open, and Michelle's department store's worth of clothes and shoes were gone. There was an envelope propped against the mirror on top of her dresser. "Kevin" was written across it in Michelle's flowy script. I went to my dresser on the other side of the bed, pulled out a gray T-shirt with a Volcom logo across the front, and managed to get it on. I turned toward the doorway. I was either going to get in my truck, start driving, and keep going until . . . something . . . or I was going to face the music, whatever that meant.

I faced the music. I stood looking down at her. It annoyed

me that she was positioned so I had to step over her to get into the kitchen. It crossed my mind that maybe the worst hadn't happened. Maybe there was time. I got down on one knee, holding my left arm against me like a broken wing, and pushed two fingers under her jaw. I knew instantly, because my stomach curdled at the coolness of her flesh, but I waited for a pulse, and waited some more, and then gave up.

I heard the noise again. I had heard it three or four times over the past ten minutes but I had been unable to make room for it in my consciousness. It was the electronic wind-chime noise that Michelle's phone made when a text came in. I looked down her body to the phone, the helpless passenger strapped against the massive backside. I reached out, took the device between thumb and forefinger, and extracted it.

There were two texts from "Sabs," which I immediately knew was a disgusting-cutesy nickname for Sabrina. The first text said, "Everything okay?" followed by a thinking emoji face. The next just said, "I'm waiting at the gas station."

I involuntarily pictured the brutal little dyke sitting in her brand new Altima that she owned for some dykey reason, parked in the lot of the Circle K that was just up the road. I had met Sabrina in passing a couple of times, and once, last winter, she had been part of the crowd when Michelle and I, and six or eight people whom Michelle knew from school, had all gone out for drinks. I thought of the young woman then as nothing more than fodder for wisecracks. With her businessman's haircut and positively adorable little face, and her rather shapeless body poured into men's work clothes, she looked like some deformed but wholesome sixteen-year-old boy hired to work at a lumberyard. She looked wholesome, that is, until you noticed the elaborate tattoo work peeking out from beneath her sleeves and collar.

A mere six months before, Michelle and I had laughed about Sabrina together as I spieled about ovaries and testosterone and any other "gendered" buzzwords I could work into my commentary. What happened in the intervening time, I still don't know. Maybe Sabrina knew tricks I never heard of, or maybe the college body-snatching operation is that refined, and Michelle was flipped, turned against her own menfolk—her own DNA—so thoroughly and so quickly that she was long gone before I got my first tremor of uncertainty.

As I stared into the void, trying to puzzle this out, I heard the sound of someone arriving, the sigh of a motor, and the popping and crunching of gravel under tires. I stood upright, momentarily re-energized, and went to the living room window. I leaned over the couch and parted the blinds, heard myself say, "*Oh, thank Christ,*" as I saw that it was just my mom, rolling up in her dust-coated, silver CRV, returning to the trailer that stood on the opposite side of the driveway.

I watched for several seconds, just to reassure myself. In the dying light, Mom got out of the vehicle, dragged a couple of reusable, eco-green grocery bags after her, and with one of those in each hand, and her purse hanging from her shoulder, she closed the car door with her knee and went up the steps to the little front porch my grandfather had built three decades ago, then disappeared inside the trailer as the headlights of the CRV automatically flicked off.

Staring at Mom, at that battered trailer and the dusty bleak world that was all I had ever known, I was knocked out of the moment, certain that I was, after all, the sick one; certain that my world was about to fall in on itself. A memory inflicted itself on me, and I was suddenly, unexpectedly, lacerated by the words Michelle had spoken in the midst of one of our endless, pointless debates a few weeks ago. "You know what you are, Kevin?" she had said, her eyes narrowed with galling detachment, looking at me like I was a laboratory specimen. "You're one of those incels. One of those guys who's just gonna freak out and start killing people one day. I didn't realize it before, because you act like Cliff, like you're a big man, but that's just an act. You show off with all your autistic knowledge of books, but you just read whatever you find. You're not *educated*. You're not *complete*. Inside, you're a frightened little boy."

Christ, I thought now, feeling my pulse ticking up, seeing myself, finally, as the pathetic cliché that Michelle and her goddamned girlfriend and goddamned professors saw. *I am nothing but the latest headline. I am* him: the *rage-driven, all-consuming, world-destroying white male. I am doomed. Because they're right . . .*

Michelle didn't even know that she'd hit the bull's eye. That was the disturbing part. I had never told her about the tantrum I'd had at nineteen, when Mom took my shitty computer away because I was down to a hundred-twenty pounds. I had never told her how I ended up strapped to a stretcher, hauled away by paramedics, and then locked in a bare room at the hospital in Holbrook while the cuts on my wrists, as shallow as cat scratches, faded to pink lines. I had certainly never copped to the second time, only five years ago, when Mom had come into my bedroom in the trailer, after the tin light fixture had torn out of the cardboard ceiling, and my three-hundred-dollar gaming chair had smashed against the paper-thin wall, and there I was on the floor, shaking and sweating, with the dollar-store extension cord around my neck.

There were no paramedics that time. That was when Mom, gagging back her feminism for once, had called in her "asshole little brother." Maybe Cliff was right, she admitted after twenty-eight years. Maybe Kevin did need a man to guide him. And that was how I found myself, the next Monday, wrestling sheets of drywall, barely able to support my half. That was how I came to be nursed along, encouraged, treated like a genius for doing stupid shit like reading a tape-measure properly and cutting a straight line with a razor knife. That was how I learned to fake normalcy, and became physically stronger, and less fearful of my fellow humans, week by week, until I could bullshit and drink beers with gruff noisy men who, to my amazement, treated me like I belonged on their job-sites in the Carhartt work pants and tool belt my uncle had bought me.

I guess there was no way to hide almost thirty years of nothing, and maybe that's what did it in the end. Maybe I had been faking life, faking even being human, and Michelle finally saw through it. Or maybe she had always seen through it, but she had been used and discarded by enough normal guys that getting with me, and eventually marrying me, had been a very pragmatic choice.

When I proposed, anyway, Michelle didn't hesitate. After

a good enough approximation of a standard wedding, in which Cliff was my best man and Mom acted like she had made it all happen, and then two weeks in Mexico, which was a wonderful time if you want to know the truth, we moved into this house that my grandmother still owned, and would own until she inevitably died in the convalescent home where she had been since her stroke. The idea was that here, Michelle didn't have to work, and could concentrate on finishing school. I was manning up, providing a home and any other type of support she needed, because that was what men did.

Lol.

3

I was collapsed onto the couch, my hands over my face, peeking through my fingers periodically at Michelle, when the single *Ding!* of the doorbell shot through my entrails like a jolt of electricity. My body went rigid and the dull ache in my shoulder sharpened in a nasty way, as if the knife was being thrust back into the open wound. I knew it was Mom. She made a point of coming over, rather than sending texts, when she had something to tell me or Michelle. It was a boomer thing. Or maybe an enlightened liberal thing. Or maybe both. She'd picked up a line somewhere about the dehumanizing effects of cell-phone culture and repeated it whenever she got the chance. The problem was that when Mom came over she usually came inside—practically forced her way in, really. She didn't like being kept on the front stoop like a solicitor.

I now did a calculation as automatically as I took my next breath. I instantly saw that even if I kept Mom outside, the angle of the opened front door drew a straight line to the kitchen entryway. I said it to myself, feeling the horrible finality of it: *to Michelle's body*. Once that door opened, it was over. Mom had a checklist of non-negotiable personal principles and high on the list was that a man never, ever, but never, raised his hand to woman. Let alone a rolling pin. I could expect no sympathy from her, no matter how I tried to explain what Michelle had done to me. *What part of "never" don't you understand?* Once I opened that door and Mom got the faintest notion of what had taken place here, the police were coming. Then I could look forward to being cuffed, shoved, pulled, escorted, treated like a snarling mutt, my brain kneaded by professional interrogators, my reality a series of procedures, courtrooms, and cages inevitably stocked with burly psychopaths who would beat the shit out of me, bully me, rape me . . . And that would be life forevermore—or if I was lucky, for the next twenty years or so.

Ding! went the doorbell. "Hello?" came Mom's voice.

I could suddenly feel the sweat like warmed-over cream-of-something soup in my armpits, running down my back, collecting in the hollow of my chest. I was panicking, but I also knew I was panicking, and a lifeline of reason, pitched from somewhere in my subconscious, emerged through the haze and slapped against my panic. That was the moment, I guess, when I committed. The next I knew I was in the kitchen and I had lifted Michelle's sneaker with my good arm, and was clutching the unfeeling ankle, heaving my weight against hers, dragging her to where she couldn't be seen from the open front door. She was loose-limbed as she slid, her right arm extended away from her body, seeming to reach toward the steak knife. When she was back far enough I gently set her leg down, stepped over and snatched up the knife, and deposited it on the counter next to the rolling pin.

I looked away, preparing to bluff mom, and realized that I had another problem. When I tried to clear my throat I could only produce a dry, helpless scrape. I stretched my mouth and my lips were sticking to my teeth. I turned and opened the fridge. It was almost fully dark outside now and I squinted at the light. There on the middle shelf, like an actor on center stage, was a final Bud tallboy wearing the plastic six-pack rings like a cape. I seized it and peeled the ring off its neck. I got it cracked, took a sip, then found myself tilting it, vacuuming the cold deliciousness down, and nearly finished it as I stood there next to the open fridge. I took a deep breath, cleared my throat successfully, and felt my mouth limber up. I was like a video game character whose life-bar had just filled back up to forty percent.

Another *Ding!* and an insistent, upward-inflecting, "Hey, Kev?" sounded from the living room.

I called, "I'm coming." Not urgent, not peeved. Just right. I took another gulp of beer and walked across the dark living room.

I twisted the knob and pulled the door toward me and said, "Hey, Mom." I held the door open just enough to not be rude, but not enough to be read as a *come on in*. It was lighter outside than it seemed it would be, but Mom's face under her dyed yellow Karen 'do was barely visible. She tilted her head a little and said, "Is everything okay over here?"

"Yeah, fine. Why?"

"The house is dark. Is Michelle home?"

"Yeah." I knew Mom must have seen her car in the carport.

"Why is—"

"We were talking, Mom. We had a fight."

If you've never been in a situation like this, I can tell you that a certain instinct kicks in. Your mouth starts coming up with plausible responses, on its own, the way your hand leaps up of its own accord when you sense something flying at you.

Now Mom said, "O-o-oh!" in a *Now it all makes sense* kind of way, and added, "Okay, then. I was just going to see what you guys are up to. Mark is coming over, and we're going to Lucky Lanes and I thought . . ."

Depending on the day, I either detest Mom utterly, admire her moronic tenacity, or I am perfectly objective, and therefore profoundly indifferent to her. You want a picture? She has the same zero-fat body type that I do, but she's got sixty years worth of creases on her face, which make a sad contrast with her fake blonde hair, fake tits, and her whole fake-hip personality. Most people see right through her act, but one thing I can say is, she will keep bluffing to the bitter end. No matter what humiliating circumstances she bumbles into—such as acquiring a homeless stalker after looking for love on Tinder, or raising a son who is a certifiable basket case—she treats it as if it was a random lighting strike, something that could happen to anyone, and her reputation, therefore, as far as she's concerned, remains beyond reproach.

"Probably not tonight," I said.

"All right," she said. "Just thought I'd check." Then she pointed and said, "What happened to you?" I followed the line of her finger, remembering the bulge from the washcloth and duct tape, and now I saw that a dark spot of blood, about the size of a half-dollar, had soaked through my Volcom T-shirt.

"Oh, that. I slipped and cut it when I was changing the air filter on my truck. It was bleeding a lot. I taped it up good. Cliff would be proud." That's how fast the machinery works. I knew not to say that it happened at work, because that lie could be exposed, accidentally, if she brought it up to Cliff. Maybe I'm that smart, or maybe I've just read too many books about these situations.

"Ouch," Mom said.

"It's no big deal." I said, and lifted the tallboy that I held in my right hand and took a swig, underscoring that thought.

"Okay, well, don't let it get infected. And you kids work out your troubles. Be nice. Never go to bed angry, you know."

"Yeah, I'll try not to."

"Hi, Michelle," she yelled past me. "*Don't worry, everything will be fine, honey.*"

We looked at each other as no answer came.

"She might be in the bathroom," I said, and Mom said okay again, and she was finally backing away, and we exchanged a couple more inanities and I got the door shut.

Like an actor in a movie pantomiming relief, I leaned my forehead on my hand against the door, just breathed for a solid minute, until I couldn't stand the ache of my pulse in my shoulder any more. *Jesus Christ*, I thought. *No turning back now.*

When I turned to walk I felt like the gravity dial had been cranked up to impossible levels, and merely standing, not just lying on the floor and flattening out, constituted a miracle of will. But I made my way to the bathroom, to do something about the blood soaking through my T-shirt, and to put on my third clean shirt of the day—this time a black one that would not show blood spots, if that came up. Whatever else was going to happen, that seemed like something that should be done.

As I walked, I heard the wind chime on Michelle's cell again, and I thought of Sabrina and wondered if I should just make a run for it.

4

This little dialogue started playing in my head. *Michelle?* I imagined myself saying to some faceless, interested party. *Michelle left. I don't know where she went. She just took off. She was packed up to leave and she got in her car and drove away and I haven't seen her since.*

I paced the house as I went over this. Bedroom, hallway, living room, peek into the kitchen, blink at the dark mass on the floor, mutter some *fucks* and *shits*, and walk the circuit again. My talk with Mom had broken some barrier in my mind. I was no longer outside myself, helplessly shaking my head at what a fool I was and how fucked I was. I was calibrated to the moment I was in. I now wished Mom would leave so I could do what needed doing. Was Mark coming to get her or was she meeting him at the bowling alley?

After about thirty minutes, when Mom hadn't left, and I

realized it might be another hour or maybe longer before she did leave, I was struck by a thought, and suddenly I didn't want her to leave. Suddenly I was in motion, determined to get in under the wire, to give her something to think about—something to know. Back in the kitchen, I was on my knees in the dark, and I gritted my teeth and probed at the trampoline-tight material of Michelle's front pockets. I found nothing, and went out the back door, into the carport, opened the driver's door of her Toyota, and saw that her car was heaped with her belongings, clothes stacked in the backseat, on top of boxes of various sizes. The passenger seat contained her laptop bag and purse, and several pairs of shoes were stuffed onto the floor in front of the seat. I saw that the keys were in the ignition.

I breathed a "*f-u-u-ck,*" as it struck me that she had been only seconds from a clean getaway when I walked in. Maybe she had gone back to deposit the letter. Maybe it was just the goddamned cat. I gave my head a violent shake, as if I could physically clear away the *what ifs*, and then I closed the car door softly and pushed on it until the dome light was extinguished.

I thought of the layout of this place, and my mind returned to the crude plan that had begun to take shape. The eastern edge of the property is defined by the little creek, and beside that creek is the dirt road, which is still used to access the farm fields, and opens up to the public road a few hundred yards from our driveway. It was a temporary solution, if even that, but I had nothing else.

Inside the back door, in the kitchen again with Michelle, I caught my breath a moment, then I straightened my back, filled my lungs, and roared, "*I don't fucking care!*" which was as likely as anything. I stormed across the living room, opened the front door, and bellowed, "*Good! Fuck you!*" and slammed the door shut with an amateur judo kick, managing to rattle the glass in the front window. Then I stalked into the kitchen, turned the carport light on, then off, opened the door and yelled, "*Leave, then! Good fucking riddance!*" My voice was slightly hoarse, almost failing me, but that was just right.

This time I stepped outside, into the dark carport, and slammed the door behind me. I stepped over to the little car, tore the door open, climbed in, and jammed my foot onto the brake. I started the motor and waited a moment with it running. My heart was slugging away, the beer trying to boil up the pipe and fill my mouth. I saw a light come on in what I knew was the master bedroom of the trailer, and I took that as my cue. I reversed the Toyota into the open portion of the driveway, my truck with its gray primer-spots sliding by beside me. I groped the control levers sprouting off the steering column, made the windshield wipers drag noisily across the glass once, and then found the headlight switch. Gravel sprayed from under the tires as I dropped it into drive and lurched it toward the street. I braked just enough to make sure I wasn't going to get T-boned, and blasted off toward the county road, managing to chirp the tires.

When I made the turn onto the county road, I pulled to the shoulder, let a car pass, and swung a U-turn, killing the headlights as I went. Now I returned to our road and veered hard to my left and jolted onto the dirt path to the farm fields. I stole along in the darkness like this, the car rocking violently in potholes a couple of times, making my head bob. To my left was the green-black, overgrown foliage which bordered the creek. Just past a lone giant oak, I cranked the steering wheel and spectral branches swept into the path of my vision, and then they were pressing against the windshield while the points of their mates tortured the little Toyota's paint with grating screeches. I gunned the gas, gently, over and over, pressing the car under the tree, into the neck-high welter of blackberry bushes, until the tires started losing traction. The last rain had been a month ago, and the ground was hard enough that I could have gotten a run at it and barreled the car right down the into the trickling water. Instead, I stopped when the wide trunk of the oak was between the car and the back of the house. Because of my useless left arm, I had to lean back and use my foot to heave the door open against the blackberry bushes, and I was fairly swimming through the spiteful, clinging leaves and razor-equipped stems for a few yards, but then I was there, staggering on the packed dirt of the farm road, under the glittering stars, dripping sweat and probably blood, and when I looked back I could not make out the car.

The thought had assailed me as I was cutting the U-turn, but I had quashed it. Now it loomed up and terrorized me. Stupid fuck me had not locked the door after Mom left. I imagined her hearing the commotion, seeing Michelle tear out of there, and then coming to the house, knocking, letting herself in, saying, "Hello? Hello?" as she intruded, until she stepped into the kitchen and hit the light switch.

"*Just mind your own fucking business, Mom,*" I muttered as

I stalked across the weedy plot—formerly Grandma's garden—that separated the farm road from the house.

Skulking like a burglar, I stepped into the empty carport. There were no windows on this side of the house, and the back door was solid, so I could not tell if there was a light on in the kitchen. I could not tell, that is, if this whole farce was over. I crossed the vacuum of space where Michelle's car had been a few minutes before, clasped the door handle, squinted, twisted it, and pushed. On the other side was darkness.

My head sagged on my neck. My body deflated with a long, hissing breath, the relief all but unbearable. I lacked the strength, it seemed, to get myself over the threshold, and get the door closed behind me, but I did it. Then I leaned against the door, slid down, and came to rest on the floor.

"Kevin-honey?" Mom said from the living room, knocking on the door that she'd already opened. "Honey, where are you?" The living-room light ignited, and poured in at a slant. Mom was inside. She would walk straight to the kitchen, hand fluttering automatically to the light switch, and see everything. I crawled, then hauled myself up, and transported myself, somehow, to the entryway of the kitchen. I propped my right shoulder against the door-frame, just in time to stop Mom in her tracks, about three feet from me in the lighted room.

"Honey?" she said, looking at me, her face contorting with exaggerated concern.

"Hey, Mom," I said.

"Did Michelle leave?"

"Yeah."

"Honey? Holy shit. Are you okay?"

I followed her gaze to my bare right arm. The arm I'd used to make my way out of the blackberry bushes. It was covered in lightly inflamed scratches, with a couple of bright red stripes. I had re-taped my shoulder, gotten several layers of material flattened pretty good against the wound, and a quick shift of my eyes told me it wasn't bleeding through this time. So there was that.

"Nothing happened," I said. "I'm fine." My voice was a monotone. The scratches, as if responding to my awareness of them, began stinging, salted by the mist of sweat. I wondered if there were sticks or leaves in my hair. I could smell the pungent organic scent on my clothes. I wondered if Mom could.

"Honey?" Mom said again. I was getting sick of hearing that. "Do you . . . want to talk?"

"No, honey," I said, "I don't, honey. Okay, honey? Fuck." I felt the hysteria coming on, like an electrical buzz expanding in my brain. Then I realized that I might be setting off alarms in her brain. Unstable . . . suicidal . . . better call someone. I cleared my throat and said, "Not right now, okay? Can you give me some space? I'm going to be fine. I'm totally fine. I just don't want to deal with anyone right now."

She took a step closer, raised a hand as if to stroke my cheek, and said, "Oh, Kev. It's going to be—"

Without making a conscious decision to, I knocked her hand away, throttling back the violence I felt just enough so it was not quite a vicious gesture. She froze as if I'd slapped her face. I said, "Please, Mom. I just want to be by myself right now. I promise, I'm fine. Can you just leave?"

Now she nodded, looking like I'd just told her of a dear one's death, and the tears started collecting in her black-outlined eyes. There's nothing, I am convinced, that women can't make about themselves. You could be blown into two halves of a man, and they will start snuffling over what's left of you, making you feel like a failure for dying in such a pathetic way, forcing you, as your last act on Earth, to form your lips into a smile and burn up your final fumes of life consoling them.

Mom bit her pink-painted bottom lip, deepened the wrinkles around her eyes, and nodded tragically. I just held my position at the entryway to the kitchen. She started babbling, called me "honey" once, caught herself the next time and changed it to "Kev," and made her way back to the front door. I didn't follow her, because I knew my knees weren't steady enough. Then she was finally outside, and she told me it was going to be fine, and that Michelle would come back, just wait. I said okay, I know, don't worry I'll be fine, yes, I hear you, we'll talk later, okay, okay . . . and then the door shut.

I turned and got myself to the sink just as my guts convulsed. I let go onto the unwashed plates, bowls and utensils, feeling Budweiser, stomach acid, and swimming bits of my afternoon chicken sandwich coming out of my nose.

After about a week of dry heaving, I scooped water from the faucet stream into my mouth, rinsed and spit a few times, then splashed the running water around with my hand to wash the orange-flecked vomit away. As happens after a system purge, some life returned to my body, and with that some clarity, if not sanity, to my mind. I looked down at the dim form of Michelle. Her phone was on the floor beside her, and the screen glowed with another incoming text.

Michelle left, I thought. *I don't know where she went.*

In the light angling in from the living room, I suddenly saw that there were spots of my blood, dried to almost the same color as the linoleum, but with a matte finish that made them too apparent when the light tried to glare off of them. I wondered if Mom had noticed, and I knew she hadn't, or she would have said something, maybe barged past me to inspect. But the thought gave me a jolt, and I quickly found a dishrag in a drawer, wet it in the sink, got onto my knees, and began scrubbing.

5

I probably haven't made clear what a nasty little being Sabrina was. It didn't have to do with her physical self. If you only considered what God had given her, she might have been considered above average. I had no idea of her ancestry until I met her half-brother—which I will tell you about soon—but the vaguely ethnic cast of her face could have, I suspect, made her beautiful. She had flawless olive skin, arched eyebrows, and full lips, and when she surprised you with a smile her assumed masculinity seemed to go up in smoke, and you were stricken by a cute set of dimples and a strangely endearing aspect of vulnerability.

The problem, of course, was that her natural charm was actually a mockery of charm. In the brief time I'd known her socially I became aware of a crude, cruel, perversely arrogant personality. I decided, the one night I had spent a couple of hours around her, that Sabrina's IQ was quite low. She had a flat, aggressive manner of speaking, the only intensifier adjective she seemed to know was "fuckin'," and she threatened, in a way that gave no indication of being a joke, to "mess up" people who bothered her.

Once, a few weeks before, when I'd told Michelle a joke that Cliff had told me—*What does a lesbian have in common with Pinocchio? They're both trying to be real boys but just end up looking like jackasses*—Michelle had remarked that I'd better not say anything like that around Sabrina unless I wanted serious trouble. That had made my male pride smart, and I had stated that a merely average man could kick the ass of the strongest woman, and I could certainly make short work of old Sabrina, and I'd like to know the last time that little cretin had unloaded thirty five-eighths drywall sheets by herself, or spent a twelve-hour day up and down a ladder, hoisting those heavy-ass sheets against ceiling joists and driving screws straight up against gravity. In response, Michelle had spoken cryptically about gang affiliations and people who crossed Sabrina being taught lessons, and I had scoffed and said that wasn't how things worked in the real world; girls weren't the enforcers because girls had soft arms and soft chests, and if there was one type of person that would have no patience with some lezbo playing tough guy it was members of street gangs.

But Michelle knew that my knowledge of such things was just the clichés and macho fantasies I'd absorbed from crime novels, and most of those written in another century, about another world. When I'd first met Michelle in Jim's Main Street Tavern—me spattered with drywall mud, the muscles

I'd finally acquired on display in my white T-shirt—I had dazzled her with my knowledge of books. She was one of the college girls from over in Antrim, slumming it with the hicks in Brunswick. She told me she was majoring in English Lit and I saw my chance and took it, played the one ace I had in this life. I had spent years—literal years—holed up in my room in the single wide, reading everything and anything. I had quit high school after my freshman year, but the library was a ten-minute walk, and the close-out shelf, where outdated and underappreciated books got released back into the wild for ten cents a pop, became my addiction. After Mom took my first computer away, just before I turned twenty, the addiction became more acute, and crime fiction became my drug of choice. I happened across *The Moving Target* by Ross Macdonald, and its effect on me was such that, over the next few years, I worked through the whole hard-boiled-noir library like the very hungry caterpillar munching through leaves. That afternoon, when Michelle and I first met—just hours before she was to take my virginity—I ended up leaning into her as we sat at the bar, delivering an impassioned, slurry screed about Chandler, Cain, Thompson, Ed McBain, both the Macdonalds . . . I explained what differentiated noir from hard-boiled, and I insisted that crime fiction is the true, enduring literature of our age because, goddamnit, it's about real people with real problems.

Michelle had pressed her tit against my arm, made me dizzy with awareness of where the situation was headed, and had done a convincing impression of having her mind blown. But, I now know, she saw her chance and was taking it, just like I was. She had found a yokel, a nerd, a poor jackass who didn't understand sexual dynamics, who had no idea that he looked like a catch. She knew that, Miss Piggy or not, she could own me.

And then, after she had me, she didn't want me. I was less of a man, as far as she was concerned, than a fucking lesbian. "Toughness isn't just lifting pieces of sheetrock," Michelle had told me. "There's also guts. That's what Sabrina has. People know not to cross her." And with that she clammed up, refused to give details. I just had the enraging sense that she was entirely sold on the idea of Sabrina being some kind of action hero.

The latest message from Sabs said, "I'm coming over." The clock now showed "7:38." The last wind chime had been fifteen minutes ago. I winced, thinking of her arriving as I spoke with my mother, or her seeing Michelle's car dive down the farm road and knowing just what had happened. But it didn't matter. I had to assume that she would come knocking any second. So I went to work.

With only one fully functional arm, I could not get Michelle upright and over my shoulder, and my attempt at the procedure resulted in her slumping grotesquely to one side, against the wall opposite the counter. In the light reflecting from the living room, I could see a glint of white between her eyelashes. I stared in fascination for several seconds as I crouched there, wondering if I was seeing signs of life, then certain that I wasn't.

I ended up painfully using both arms, pulling her by the ankles, leaning at a hundred-thirty degrees. I dragged her out of the kitchen, through the living room, down the hall and into the second bedroom, and sealed her inside. The doorknobs in the house all had interior locks. Once I set the mechanism and closed the door, it could not be opened from the outside, except by jimmying a piece of wire through a hole on the front of the handle. After a moment of staring I simply left her, face-down, on the carpet beside my battered and drink-ringed computer desk, and my old office chair. The closet was crammed with my junk. The clock was ticking. This was the best I could do. I backed into the hall and pulled the door until I felt the *click*. Then I stepped across to the bathroom, hit the light switch, and checked my appearance. Except for looking wasted and bloodless, I could pass for normal. There were no leaves or twigs in my hair, and I ran water on my hand and finger-combed it. I put on deodorant and found I could barely lift my left arm. Except for a couple of bright lines, the scratches on my right arm had calmed to a faint redness.

There is a sense of recklessness that is what? Wonderful? Exhilarating? Those words are probably too strong. Maybe just liberating. There is an amount of inner peace, tinged with excitement, that takes you when you have no choice but to throw the dice. I was ready, I thought, for Sabrina to show up. I didn't know what was happening with my life after that, but I was almost eager to face my rival.

In the interest strictly of sustenance, I went to the kitchen and rummaged, came up with some cheese, mayonnaise, and mildly stale saltines, and ate about fifteen little sandwiches, washing them down as I went with milk chugged out of the carton. The clock now said "8:35," and I began to feel a new, nagging concern. I imagined Sabrina knowing, having already been here and left, having already called to the police. Then I argued myself out of that with the idea that the police, if they had been called, would be here right now. So what was taking her so long?

I entertained a few dim speculations about a week or a month from now. What happened when Michelle never turned up? What would everybody think? Wasn't I just delaying, and worsening, the inevitable? But the idea of calling the police myself, becoming a headline, a segment on a low-quality true crime series, fodder for breathless local gossip, was unacceptable. *There was always something off about that guy. I heard he tried to hang himself.* If I had just taken the one wild swing with the goddamned rolling pin, if the rage had not throttled up higher and higher as my blood trickled out and her words looped in my head, I might have my shoulder properly stitched up, and even claimed self-defense. We might have stalemated, and gone our separate ways with our gouges and lumps, and I would still have a life to rebuild.

Stop, I told myself.

And then I had no choice.

The knock sounded right beside me, or anyway, only ten feet from me. It was at the carport door, and it was aggressive. The first set of raps was knuckles, but those apparently did not have the right energy, so the next three were thumps made by a fist, hard enough to rattle the door in its frame.

I glanced at the floor, to see if I had left any stray spots of blood, and saw the thing that I had been working around, shoving out of the way, ignoring: Michelle's baby-blue backpack, packed to full-term pregnancy, waiting to tell of my guilt. It was sitting upright against the cabinet. I admonished myself through my teeth, saying, "*You fucking blind fucking imbecile,*" as I snatched the thing up, and stepped over and swung it into the darkened living room, so it came to rest under the wall-mounted TV.

I looked at the door to the carport. I felt like I was in a dream as I moved toward it. One second I would be in here, all alone and safe, and then it would be show-time; I would be an actor in a cheap drama, playing opposite the perverted little demon that had crept up from its chamber of hell and stolen my wife.

I flicked on the carport light, opened the door and looked down at Sabrina. There was a one-step drop into the carport, and she was glaring up at me from a foot-and-a-half disadvantage. The soft-edged, good-looking adolescent boy's face was a blank challenge. She wore a black vest over a black T-shirt, trying to kid the world that she didn't have tits. "Where'd Michelle go?" she said. Her voice was a woman's voice, but she tried to flatten it out, pitch it low enough to be male, and managed to sound like a woman impersonating a child impersonating a man. I understood, somehow, that she had pulled in looking for Michelle's car in the carport, and then gotten out of her car and walked into the carport, in a state of confusion, as if Michelle's car might be hiding in a corner somewhere. Then, accepting that Michelle wasn't here, she had begun thumping on the nearest door.

I said, "Michelle left. I don't know where she went." I found that there was a smile pulling at the sides of my mouth, a swell of mirth trying to grow into a laugh in my chest. I had no fucking idea why—but then, I knew exactly why. I had been designated the loser in all this, but I had taken all their dreams down with me.

Sabrina was nodding, her face stony. She cut a look to her left, out toward the driveway. Finally she said, "That don't make sense."

"What *doesn't* make sense?" I said, enunciating the correct grammar.

She twitched a little, filled her lungs, tilted her head back and drilled her gaze into mine. "She isn't answering my texts. Where'd she go?"

"She didn't tell me, Sabrina. She left me."

"Why isn't she answering my texts?"

"How the fuck do I know?"

"What the fuck are you smirking about?" she said, raising her voice in a startling way. That was when Roxy's yell sounded. The cat had heard a voice other than mine, and probably thought it might be Michelle, and came to demand food. I looked over my shoulder and saw the animal standing uncertainly, looking at Sabrina with its standard commingling of curiosity and contempt. I looked back to see Sabrina's face slackened with shock, contemplating the cat. She raised her eyes to me and stabbed her finger into the kitchen. She said, "She was bringing that fuckin' cat! Why'd she leave it here?" and with that declaration she came alive, agitated by her own agitation, and lowered her head and tried to shove me aside and step up into the house.

I heard myself calmly saying, "No," as I braced my right arm against the doorjamb. Sabrina sort of butted against the arm and then stepped back into the carport. "Michelle left in a hurry." I explained in a matter-of-fact tone. "The cat was outside somewhere so she couldn't take it. I'm sure she's planning on coming back for it."

Sabrina's nostrils were flared, her body moving with her breathing, her eyes blinking rapidly. She looked from me to the cat and then back to me. She actually opened and closed her right hand, as if readying her fist, preparing to take me out with one punch.

I said, "I know everything. Michelle told me all about you two. I don't want anything to do with this shit-show. Why don't you just take off?"

She continued to glower. I maintained my aloof expression. It was foolish, but I was taking my revenge where I could.

"We'll see about this," she finally said. "You better fuckin' hope I don't have to come back here."

"Oh, I'm hoping," I said as she began to turn away.

"Smart ass!" she yelped suddenly, turning back to me, pointing at me with her child's hand. "This ain't a fuckin' joke. I don't like how you're acting."

There was, to tell the truth, something particularly unsettling about her frankness. She didn't have the imagination for psychological warfare. She didn't try to sow fear and doubt in her adversary. If she informed you that she was coming for you, it was a safe bet that she had decided to come for you, and you had better plan accordingly.

But I just kept looking at her. Giving her nothing. Holding her in limbo. She said, "We'll see if you keep smirking, motherfucker," and strutted out of the carport, a fearless bantam hen, with a bantam hen's brainpower. A few seconds later I heard the door shut on her pristine little car—a car that I would come to know intimately—and heard the nearly silent motor start up. The headlights bounced off objects as the vehicle swung in an arc, rolled back onto the pavement, and growled away.

I heard the wind chime and was amazed, when I turned around and closed the door, to see that Michelle's cell was on the counter. I walked to it. There was another text from Sabs. Just sent. "WHERE ARE YOU?" She must have rocked her car to a halt on the shoulder, her mind scrambled, and fired it off in desperation.

I was staring at the phone when the screen switched to incoming call mode, and began playing another type of wind-chime simulation, showing "Sabs" as the caller. I knew that the phone represented a major problem. The ringtone stopped before it could go to voicemail, and immediately started again. I placed my hand over the phone and held the button until the power-down icon showed, and I swiped it. Something would have to be done about this device.

Ten o'clock and then eleven o'clock came. I darkened the house and sat on the couch and thought. At first I was convinced that Sabrina would call the police after seeing the cat, and I resigned myself to it if that was my fate. But after an hour passed I realized that she probably didn't even consider it. Maybe it was the Black Lives Matter thing. The police were the enemy, and they would just cover for me, or believe whatever came out of my white male mouth. Maybe she just couldn't put the puzzle pieces together properly.

Eventually, my thoughts became distant voices, and I swung my feet up, laid my head on a throw pillow, and let my body power down. Sleep was a carnival of nightmares that passed through the looking glass of consciousness, remained my reality when I awakened, and took on more sinister and insane shapes when I managed to sink back into unconsciousness. In the deadest hours, when the world was perfectly still, my eyes flipped open, a fantastic horror gripping me. There was a sickly glow of fever in my skull, nausea roiling in my stomach, and my whole left arm felt as if it had been injected with a syringeful of poison. Before the notion was fully formed I had crawled off the couch and was staggering through the house.

I had never sterilized the wound, and when I got my shirt off and peeled away the covering in front of the bathroom mirror, a dark, angry red was blossoming around the shadowed scarlet of the opening. I took the rubbing alcohol from the medicine cabinet, folded my left hand to the shoulder and pinched the skin so the little mouth opened, and used my right hand to pour the stuff in, unconcerned that it dribbled down my body and under the waistline of my pants. I clenched my jaw and relished the searing pain. You can enjoy anything, in a way, if you imagine it's doing you good. I went to the bedroom, fetched a sock from the top drawer of my dresser, got it sopping with rubbing alcohol, and laid down, this time on the bed, with the sock on the wound, and a pillow laid on the sock, to hold it in place.

I didn't know anything else until the morning, when I woke up and realized that Sabrina was in the room with me.

6

My second sleep session that night was more a form of paralysis than sleep. My brain was effectively dead until a basic organism instinct activated it, made me aware of *breathing* in my immediate vicinity. I lay on the bed that Michelle and I had shared, the blankets covering my legs, my naked torso exposed, the alcohol-soaked sock fallen away so the wound on my shoulder was apparent.

I had not closed the blinds the previous evening, and my eyes opened to the glare of daylight and the blurred form of Sabrina looming over me. I muttered, "What the fuck!" and felt my eyes go wide, and the lesbian just stared at me with her peculiar, guileless, blankness.

"Where is she, dude?" Sabrina said.

I began sitting up, and managed to say, "Get the fuck out—" when Sabrina put the point of a knife to my throat.

She tilted her torso back and held the weapon at the end of a straightened arm, with the tip pressing into my skin. I went rigid. Her eyes were luminous, glassy in the morning light, empty of emotion. I noticed for the first time that they were green. She said, "You got that cut on your shoulder. Looks like a knife cut. And the fuckin' cat's still here. Michelle wouldn't leave the cat. You better tell me what the fuck is going on."

I stared at her. I opened my mouth but I think I only said, "Uh . . ."

She increased the pressure on the knife point, causing me to draw back, compressing the pillow under my head. I couldn't tell what kind of knife it was. I could only see that the handle was black and the blade silver. My legs, still under the covers, might as well have been tied down.

Finally I said, "We were yelling at each other and the back door was open and the cat ran off. She couldn't take the fucking cat. Come on, get that thing off my neck." It sounded like someone else speaking. I had no idea where the cool persuasiveness came from.

She just looked at me, momentarily defeated, but she kept me pinned by the knife point. Her eyes sockets were slightly raccooned. Her face was drawn. She looked like she hadn't slept in a week. She was wearing exactly what she'd been wearing the previous night. I kept staring into that tortured boy-girl countenance and she stared back, her concentration absolute, her eyes blinking rhythmically, as if I was a riveting TV show.

In *The Sea Wolf,* Jack London talks about the "courage of cowardice"—the way a guy who is truly terrified will do remarkable things, take action in ways that a braver man wouldn't be driven to. I learned that morning that there is such a thing as the shrewdness of stupidity—the way a person whose mind is not cluttered by possibilities and speculations will lock onto an obvious truth while everyone else is in a haze of uncertainty. Sabrina blinked once, contorted her lips like a slow reader working through a paragraph, and said, "She's here."

I said, "What?" but the lesbian had already whipped the knife away and turned around. She stepped out of the bedroom and I sat up in time to see her shove the door and flick on the light in the bathroom, where my two bloody, discarded T-shirts were strewn, and the open bottle of rubbing alcohol stood on the counter—which was spattered, in a gaudy way, with my blood, as was the sink. I heard her say, "Motherfucker!" and then I heard the door scrape open in the bath stall, as she checked to see if I'd hidden the body there.

I was on my feet now. I still wore the work pants I'd pulled on yesterday morning. I did not realize until later, when I was able to reflect on all this, that my left arm had become mobile again and whatever sickness had begun working in my system had gone into remission. The sterilization had worked wonders, it seemed.

Sabrina emerged from the bathroom and went directly to the closed door of the second bedroom. I found myself paralyzed as I watched her try the knob. Then her eyes grew wide and she was stepping backward and I heard myself roar "HEY!" as I realized what she was doing. With a weird fluid grace, her knee hoisted to her chest, the knife flashed in an arc as her arms swung down for leverage, and she fired a black boot right into the doorknob. The wood and metal gave an explosive crunch as the door came free. It was as if she'd done the maneuver a thousand times. She hurled her weight after her leg, practically tumbling into the room, catching the wall to stop her momentum. I was now moving to stop her, still playing the innocent fool, saying, "Hey! Hey! What the fuck! Hey, stop!" But I was a beat too late. The blinds in the room were closed, but she instinctively slapped the wall where the light switch should be—and was—and I heard her gasp in a way that was pure female.

I froze as she passed inside, and then it became too silent. When I reached the door, she was crouched over Michelle's well-lit body and had her cell phone in her left hand. I watched her open her right hand and let the knife fall so she could work the phone, and I dove for the device, knocking her off balance, causing her to roll onto Michelle's cool, stiffening, jean-clad legs.

Then we were both gripping the device like two kids in a silent, frantic struggle over a disputed toy. I was on top, though, and this forced her to struggle against being pinned as well as try to keep both hands on the phone. When the thing began to slip from her surprisingly vice-like clutches, she convulsed and tried to plant a knee in my crotch. This did not have the desired, Hollywood effect of incapacitating me, because she had no real leverage, but it had the undesired effect of prompting me to let go with my right hand and wallop her in the face, which caused her grip on the phone to slacken.

I immediately lifted the thing over my head, out of range of her hands, and heaved backward off of her, as we glared into each other's eyes. I had a fleeting pang of pity, seeing her down there with no proper card to play, neither a tough male nor a helpless female. But as I thought this, her eyes jerked downward and her hand slapped onto the black handle of the knife.

She rolled forward and pushed herself up with her free arm. Her face looked damp and a lock from the bangs of her young-Republican haircut curled down onto her forehead in a way that might have been stylish in another reality. The flesh under her left eye was already slightly puffed and darkened. She came toward me in a tiger crouch, leading with the knife. She didn't bother with any declarations or demands, just glared into my eyes and advanced.

Foolishly, I backed toward the bedroom, where I could be cornered, and she followed me, step by step. Her mind, it seemed, was empty of anything except puncturing me with that knife. I said, "L-listen, it-it was an accident. See my shoulder? She *stabbed* me, Sabrina!"

At this she made a strange, almost humorous face, and shook her head as if deciding against something. I stepped into the bedroom, with the queen-sized bed dominating the floor space a few feet behind me. Something, at this moment, compelled Sabrina to charge. As a matter of reflex I tried, and failed, to get the bedroom door shut against her advance.

She had the very simple goal of forcing her body through that passage, and once inside, *winning*—carving up a white male—avenging, dominating, becoming a legend in lesbian lore. I don't, of course, know if she thought anything like this, but that was what the glint in her eye said to me.

I found myself with a foot braced against the bed, attempting to force the door shut against her weight. But as it happened, in the scramble, she led with her knife arm, which ended up flattened against the wall inside the bedroom, as she worked her right leg—and would soon work the rest of her body—in after it. The bed, it turned out, provided me only an illusion of bracing. The mattress instantly began sliding off toward the opposite wall, and the frame began skating away on the laminate flooring. So I did the only thing I could do, which was abandon the door and seize the arm that held the knife.

Now I did not struggle against Sabrina. Now there was only that arm, and that knife, and my back was to the small woman as my fingers pushed deep into the flesh of her wrist and crushed the birdlike bones of her hand. I spun, drawing her into the room with me, squeezing and pulling as if I had caught a serpent that would whip back and sink its fangs into me if I was ever to let my advantage wane. I made it a full three-hundred-sixty degrees and kept going, straining every muscle, and the differences in our God-given sex-attributes became undeniable as Sabrina swung behind me as helpless as if she was caught in a machine. The serpent finally died in my grip, the knife dropped from the tiny curled fingers, and my brain registered the quiet clack of it hitting the floor, amid our duet of hoarse breaths.

Some muscle memory of long-ago playground tactics caused me to then wind Sabrina's arm up behind her back, and I drove my shoulder into her so she was pressed face-first against the wall, and my face was against her damp neck, my nose filling with the dank sweet scent of her exertion and fear. I was wheezing into her ear, begging her just to stop fighting, when she swung her head around, snarling, and attempted to bite my face. No sooner had I leaned out of range than she began calling out, "*Help! Somebody! Help me! Hey, help me!*" She worked to maintain her masculine speech, but as she increased her volume, her voice pitched higher and higher.

I had no choice then but to pull her away from the wall and drive her into it again, knocking the wind out of her—and to repeat the action until she began to sag. And then she was beneath me, struggling on the floor, but with most of the fight gone out of her. Her green eyes bulged, looking through me in stupid animal panic, and her fingers were too weak to bother my hands and wrists, which were engorged with blood, and looked gnarled and monstrous contrasted with the delicate skin of her throat. There was blood on her face, the red spots multiplying and growing, and I understood that my shoulder had begun leaking again.

But I couldn't worry about that. I couldn't stop what I was doing.

7

Dawn was growing in the corner of the sky. I figured I had better get inside. Saturday had become Sunday, and the occasional pair of headlights came off the county road and glided toward Holbrook in the misty air. I could smell myself, and I could feel two days of stale, acrid sweat dried on my body, and the grime of ancient dust, mildew and sawdust ground into my skin and coating my hair and clothes. The hole in my shoulder and the dozens of nicks I had acquired had given up aching, anesthetized, somehow, by the twenty or so hours of unrelenting mental and physical strain.

Back when this little corner of land was mated to the agricultural fields that still abutted it, the barn I stood looking at had been some kind of tractor garage. There were fifty-five-gallon drums of fifty-year-old motor oil in one of the corners, and work benches constructed from rough-hewn old redwood along the opposite wall. The structure's shell of redwood planking was worn to a nondescript gray, the tin roof leprous with rust, and the whole thing settled so far off square that the large sliding door was cinched permanently shut by the structure's weight, while the man-sized door was stuck permanently open.

At eight or nine last night, that situation had brought me a few minutes of crushing despair, but I had breathed deeply, accepted the challenge, sat on my haunches amid the tree branches that now crowded against the barn, and concocted an alternate plan. I had wrenched exactly twelve planks off the side of the structure, run the large, silver 1970s skill saw—which I purchased at the flea market earlier, when I got back from the coast—through the ancient work bench, and wound up with an opening that two little Jap sedans could be driven right through. Then I had hammered what was left of the original nails back through the planks, next to, rather than through, the original holes so they grabbed anew. Where the nails failed I used two-inch drywall screws, whose black heads became invisible when I drove them deep enough.

Anyone who happened to look at this barn yesterday, even if they had given it a close inspection, would not see anything different today. And if they leaned up to peer between the planks, they would see only the blackest black. I had picked up a roll of tarpaper and stapled it along the interior walls, up and down every inch, and then across horizontally, until I came to the cardboard tube in the center, which I would burn when I got to the burning stage of my plan.

If I didn't fall to pieces, get tripped up, get caught—at least not immediately—I had Cliff to thank. His eternal mantra was, simply, "A man works." He would say it any time a job seemed excruciatingly tedious, which happens frequently with drywall, or any time I started to sulk and lose momentum, which happened frequently when I'd first become his helper. "You want to be treated like a man?" he'd say to me. "Talk to me at the end of the day. Let's see what you got done. You ain't gonna get respect in this world pulling your pud in front of your fuckin' computer." The first week I worked for him, he'd seen the muted panic in my eyes when I'd looked at a vast room of bare wall-frame we were to sheet. I could not bear the thought of being there all day, going through the eternity of steps, over and over and over. He had not tried to lecture me or cajole me, however. He had grabbed a putty knife, uncovered some wet mud, lifted a large glob, and flung it into my face. "You like that?" he'd said, as I cursed at him and dug the material out of my eye—as I almost, I shudder to recall, began crying. "It's like being spit on, but worse, right? That ain't me, Kevin. That's the world. That's what you're gonna get from the world if you keep being a little faggot. Now let's get started, and you look like you want to be here or it's gonna get worse and worse for you. Not just with me. With your whole fuckin' life."

At the end of the day, when I looked with satisfaction at what we had accomplished, and he saw it on my face, he'd handed me a putty knife heaped with wet mud. "Go ahead, get me back," he'd said, squinting and leaning his head away in comical anticipation. I could not bring myself to do it then, but a week or two later, when he was teasing me, accusing me of being a virgin as we applied corner beads, I had nailed him in the side of the head with a nice, runny glob, and he'd grinned as he dug the stuff out of his ear and blinked it out of his eye, and said, "Motherfucker! Okay, that was your Get Out of Jail Free card. We're even. Unless you start being a faggot again."

But over the past five years he had cured me, for all time, of being a faggot. He had taught me to see work—real work—as a thing you do to get to where you want to be, rather than some kind of torture regimen. I learned, in fact, to enjoy the tedium, to take pleasure in doing little things right just for the thrill of standing back, eventually, and looking at the big thing.

There was no joy in what I did today, but there was no self-pity in it either. What was important was what got done. I had even faced down Roxy, on my knees with her in the barn, looking into the big wet yellow eyes as I readied the claw end of my hammer. I would certainly take no pleasure in murdering Michelle's cat, and as it turned out, I could not do it cold-bloodedly, any more than I could cold-bloodedly fling a glob of drywall mud into Cliff's face. I finally lowered the hammer, and petted the animal's head, and laughed out the tension and cursed myself.

Instead, Roxy rode with me to the coast, where she was to be released without her collar or tag. But in the last third of the journey, along a twisting wooded stretch, the cat had committed suicide. She had yowled at me from the moment we left, hating the strange vibrating room, and she finally hopped up behind my head. I only rolled the window down to let her feel the whoosh of air, so she would know that she didn't want what she thought she wanted. But Roxy had simply stepped over and hopped out.

What happens to a cat tumbling onto pavement at fifty miles an hour I don't know, and I almost piled my Ranger into the trunk of a pine as I peered into the rearview, but I skittered my tires straight and kept going. All I know is that she was not on the road on my return trip.

When I reached the Pacific Ocean via the overcast, windblasted town of Leonard, I parked along an inconspicuous curb and dragged myself inconspicuously to the passenger's side of my truck. Then, on the floor in front of me, leaning so my forehead was against the dash, I set the two cell phones on a large dirty stone I had brought, and used my hammer to smash them to fragments. They had to be smashed here. I had seen enough true-crime shows, and I knew there was something about how the cell towers ping the devices and track locations. So Michelle and Sabrina had driven to the coast. Although I didn't know this with any certainty. All Kevin Chapman would ever be able to tell anyone was that his wife had left him, and had apparently taken her cat.

With the fragments of phone stuffed in my jacket pockets, a cap pulled down to my eyebrows, and looking at the world through the dim window of my sunglasses, I had sauntered out onto the pier, leaning into the unrelenting wind, and thrown the bits of plastic and glass over the railing like seagull food. I watched the debris flip and tumble into the churning, opaque, glittering water, and a couple of seagulls actually did reconnaissance missions, seeing if I was in fact dropping anything edible.

Then I had driven back, not directly home, but to the flea market in Brunswick, which is the weekend identity of the town's single, rundown, self-storage facility. There I spent half of the hundred-sixty bucks that was saved up in my sock drawer on mismatched, battered, decades-old Craftsman tools and gleaming new Chinese socket sets made of metal as soft as wood.

I bought everything I figured I would need to start dismantling two little cars.

As I finally headed home, with the sun on the descent in a blue sky and a Rockstar energy drink between my legs, I had the sense that I was hallucinating. I felt nothing but an abstract curiosity about whether the cops would be waiting for me. No small part of me wanted to be released from this charade, to salvage my sanity, to tell someone, anyone, the whole truth. I became convinced, as I drove, that I would come home to crime-scene tape enwrapping my house—and, of course, strung back and forth over by the creek.

Before I left, I had driven Sabrina's Altima out to the street, and then turned right and jolted the vehicle down the farm road, and then cranked the wheel left and mashed it in among the blackberries, next to Michelle's Toyota. It was a ridiculous risk. Half a dozen cars had passed as I did it. But the only other option was to leave the Altima where Sabrina had left it, nosed up to the front of my house.

I had watched for passing cars, and when there were none I had broken off the leafiest branches I could reach and layered them over the two sedans. But the sedans were all glossy paint and glass, and it was broad daylight. Anyone who bothered to look—anyone who even glanced that way, it seemed—would see them.

And then there was the real wickedness. Once the cars were investigated, the lovers would be no trouble to find. They lay together like the final scene of Romeo and Juliet, in the darkness of the second bedroom, whose door no longer even locked.

But I came home to nothing but the bland, neglected little house that my granddad had purchased thirty-some years ago, sitting across the drive from the long, dingy, tan-and-white eyesore of the single-wide, which he'd installed for Mom and her bastard baby son shortly after he and Grandma had moved into their new house. Mom wasn't even home today. Of course she wasn't. She always spent Saturday nights playing house with Mark, the lumbering divorcé who was a decade younger than her and had a nice place out in East Holbrook.

Nothing was disturbed. I was not suspected—yet—but through the kitchen window, in the slanting rays of sunlight, I could make out the glints of the cars over by the creek. I drank down the last of my Rockstar, thought about that old tractor barn, and muttered to myself, "A man works."

8

It was two days after that, on Tuesday evening, when my cell phone came alive on the coffee table, and I picked it up and looked at the strange number, feeling a vague sense of dread. I almost red-buttoned it, but I had to do what I would do under normal circumstances, so I took a deep breath and thumbed the green icon, clapped the device to my head, and said "Hello?"

"Hello, Kevin, this is Olivia," the voice said, and I wished I had gone with my first impulse.

"Oh, hi," I answered, my pulse now trotting, straining to break into a gallop. I inhaled and held my breath, fighting down the physical and mental turmoil.

"I'm calling about Michelle," Michelle's mother said. "Her cell phone is just going to voice mail. I'm slightly concerned."

Michelle's mother is not like my mother. She does not get what she wants through blatant pressure tactics. Practically everything remains unsaid with Mrs. Caruso. Long pauses and pregnant looks let you know you're not impressing her. She gets the same effect, for that matter, with polite smiles and nods, and even with the encouraging words she manages to recite from time to time. She somehow puts everyone in the position of trying to please her and forever coming up short.

For a second I was only able to get out an "Uh . . ." I didn't know what she knew. Had Michelle informed her mother that she was now a lesbian? What would Olivia Caruso think of that development? Would she see the oppression-battling Sabrina as an improvement over the white, male drywall bum? She had been, and to an extent still was, obsessed with Trump. In fact, the only time I had ever seen her break character, and really light up with passion, was when she discussed how that son of a bitch—her words—was tearing the country apart.

I finally said, "Michelle left me. I don't know if you know . . ."

"I know, Kevin. She was supposed to call me. Afterward."

"Oh." I felt something dark and wild stir inside me. Olivia just waited. I said, "I have no idea. Do you know the whole story? Do you know . . . who she left me for?"

"I do. I can't reach her, either."

The dark, wild feeling sharpened. "I don't know what to tell you," I said. "She's gone." Only in the next second did I regret my choice of words.

"I see," Olivia said flatly. Then she just waited.

After a few beats I said, "She took all her stuff. She was pretty much cleared out when I came home on Friday."

I heard Olivia sigh, and I thought suddenly how vile the situation was. Me, the abandoned husband, was barely rating an afterthought.

She seemed to make exactly the same calculation, and said, "How are you doing, Kevin? Are you okay?"

This was more surprising than if she had just come out and accused me of killing her daughter in a fit of rage. I thought a moment, exhaled, and said, "I don't know how I'm doing. I guess I'm kind of in shock."

"I guess you would be," she said, almost to herself, and then seemed to recover again and added, "I'm sorry about this, Kevin. I know it must be very hard on you."

I sighed and said, "Yeah . . . " as much as to say, *It is, but I must keep going.*

"Well, I hope you are bearing up. Life is like this sometimes. I think everything will work out for the best."

"Yeah, I guess so," I said.

"I assume that I will hear from Michelle soon. I just wanted to see if you could tell me anything helpful. You stay strong. We do care about you, Luke and I."

Bullshit, I thought. "Okay," I said. "Thank you."

"Goodbye for now."

"Goodbye."

I took the opportunity to attach "Olivia Caruso" to the number in my cell phone. I had never had occasion to talk to her on the phone before. I guessed she had made a point, some time over the past year or two, of getting my number from Michelle. She was that kind of person. Quietly collecting everyone's vital statistics.

Two days later, when she called again, I was able to glare

at her name and attempt, and fail, to mentally prepare before I touched the green icon and raised the phone to my head.

"Hi, Olivia," I said.

"Hi, Kevin. I'm sorry to keep bothering you. I need to ask: Did you speak to Michelle before she left? I still can't reach her."

"I mean . . ." I said, stalling, scrambling for an answer that wouldn't end up contradicting anything. I remembered what my mom had witnessed and said, "Yeah. We talked. Not for very long. She left me a note, she had already packed all her stuff, and she got in her car and left."

"You talked," she said, making it sound like I had confessed to something. "And she left you a note. What did her note say?"

I blinked, looking down at my boots. "I, uh, haven't read it yet." The note, in fact, was still propped on the dresser in the bedroom, the envelope unopened. "Since we talked," I said, "since she told me what she had to say, I didn't feel like reading the same stuff, you know?" This was true enough. The note, in my mind, had been rendered irrelevant by events.

"Kevin?" Olivia's voice was suddenly slightly thick, slightly unsteady. "Can I ask you to read that note? I would like to know if it gives any indication of where Michelle might be. I'm starting to get very worried."

"Now?" My voice wasn't entirely under control.

"Please."

"I'm kind of . . . afraid to," I said. "Can I call you back in a few minutes?"

"Yes."

"Okay. I'm going to read it now."

We ended the call. I left my phone on the arm of the couch and went to the bedroom. I picked up the envelope from the dresser and sat on the bed. It occurred to me that it was exactly the same time of day that all of this had begun. The time of day I would be reading the note as Michelle intended, if I had not come home early, or if she had not lingered too long. My mind sought out symmetry, hidden meaning, but it was just coincidence. I pulled out the note, unfolded it, and set the envelope on the bed. It had been typed on a computer and then printed out. The digital file was doubtlessly in Michelle's laptop in her car. But nobody would ever have the opportunity to discover that. I narrowed my eyes and felt nothing as I read.

Kevin,

You can see that I've left. Yes, it's for good, and I doubt it comes as too much of a shock. I'm sure you are aware of the changes I have undergone. Getting married was a mistake. I didn't know who I was, and I didn't understand so much about the world. I know what you think of subjects like privilege, racism, and sexism, but I have come to understand how important these things are, and I could not just continue with the life we had started. I ask you, as a friend if no longer a lover or spouse, to please let me go. Don't try to stop this. It won't do either of us any good. I intend to legally end our marriage with no strings attached. I don't want anything from you. I might as well tell you that I am going to be living with Sabrina, as her life partner. I know what you think about that too, but I have to follow my heart. It may comfort you to know that Sabrina and I are going to move away. There will be no risk of you and I running into each other. Hopefully we can both forget this mistake and find what we both want and need.

M

I stared at the page and thought of Michelle working on assignments. I wondered if this short letter represented an hour of Michelle agonizing over words—working out and then deleting whole paragraphs, the way she used to do for her instructors—or if for me, a thing being disposed of, she had just puked it onto the digital page as quickly as her little fingers could type it, and then clicked *print*. I wondered if she had run any of it by Sabrina, the way she used to use me as a sounding board, or if Sabrina, despite being in college, could possibly help anyone compose thoughts or decide to include or leave out some phrase or idea based on any sort of nuance. I grunted at the thought of Sabrina as an editor. She was as likely to know the difference between "brisk" and "brusque" as she was to pilot the fucking space shuttle.

I went back to the couch with the letter in my hand, picked up my cell, and called Olivia Caruso back. She answered before the pseudo-ring sounded in my ear.

After perfunctory hellos, I said, "It says in the letter that she and Sabrina are moving away, and that she and I won't be running into each other. That could explain it. They must have driven somewhere already." I breathed a little harder as I spoke. As far as Olivia knew I might be crying but trying not to show it.

"But, Kevin, I should be able to reach her."

Her tone was slightly pleading. We had, bizarrely, become allies in this thing. I said, "It's spring break. They could just be camping or something, and out of cell phone range."

I could feel the tension let out of Olivia Caruso. "Yes," she breathed. "That would make sense. That has to be it. Thank you, Kevin. A mother, you know . . . The imagination starts running wild. And this is such an unusual situation."

"I understand."

I felt absurdly noble for a moment, and then deeply ashamed, and then I recalled how this woman was supporting her daughter destroying a marriage for the sake of not just a fling, but a lesbian fling, and I felt nothing more than the cold regret you feel when a rat trap catches just the arm or nose-tip of the rodent and now you have to watch its pathetic struggles. The humane thing is to find something heavy and get it over with, but the easiest course is to leave it until the next day, and hope shock or cold, or whatever, has done the job when you return.

"I'm sorry to bother you again," Olivia said. Then she blindsided me again. "How are you holding up, Kevin?"

Holding up? My mind flashed over the barn and the cars, and a few images of insane and guilt-inducing gore gripped me, and I had to shake my head clear. I said, "I'm gonna make it, I guess."

"You will make it," Olivia said. "Don't worry."

We said our parting words, and she said she was sure everything was fine, and I agreed with her, and the call was ended.

But I knew we would be talking again soon.

9

Maybe I was being a faggot, after all, and my shoulder was not cut as deeply as I was certain it was, or maybe the nature of a wound like that, neatly separating strings of muscle, is to heal up quickly if it is not infected. After it opened anew and began trickling out blood—as I rolled off Sabrina and knew that was over—I filled the bathtub and poured half a squeeze-bottle of dishwashing liquid into it, and soaked in there for an hour, refreshing the hot water regularly with my foot, sterilizing my whole body. Then I rinsed in the shower and redressed the wound, this time with a cut-up sock held fast with more duct tape, flat enough to be undetectable in a T-shirt. After that my shoulder, and the minor cuts on my right arm, and the crescent-moon gouges from Sabrina's fingernails on my wrists, seemed to instantly be on the mend. When I returned from the flea market and maniacally exerted myself, working straight through to Sunday morning, the shoulder was a constant annoyance, but no longer anything like crippling.

On Sunday, I could kid myself that I was whole again. I went to the McCann's and got a deli sandwich and some groceries, and went to bed at nine with all the doors locked and Michelle and Sabrina in the second bedroom.

On Monday morning, I drove out to Cliff's house, parked my truck next to his, and rode with him to the day's work as I usually did. I got through the day without wincing so frequently or obviously that he knew anything was wrong. Or so I figured. Luckily, we were in the latter stages of this particular job, with just sanding, vacuuming, and shooting and knocking down texture left to do, so I wasn't hoisting anything heavier than bags of joint-compound mix, and practically everything I did was exclusively or mainly with my right arm.

Cliff was sick of politics, being as it was between elections, with nothing for us right-wing fascists to do but lick our wounds and grouse about being massacred in the political and culture war. So he put a CD in his white-spattered boom box and reenacted his life in the 1980s, bobbing his hoary head to Black Sabbath and chain-drinking silver bullets from the secret cooler, which was a five-gallon mud-bucket rinsed out and filled with ice. If a client, or anyone else, happened to arrive, the can in hand could be set aside inconspicuously, draped with a rag or deposited behind the compressor, and nobody suspected that we were working on a twelve-pack.

Cliff is much more a beer guy than a pot guy—although

he is that too—and his tolerance is such that he has to really make a job of it to get drunk. He could go through a twelve-pack in a work day, and besides being a little more talkative, a little more likely to burst into song, and a little sillier in his humor, seem no different than he did on a day when he only drank coffee. I had to pace myself, because I could end up clumsy and dim-witted, and spend half the day redoing basic things, especially this time of year, before the hundred-degree days were upon us and I sweat the beer out as fast as I could drink it.

Cliff likes dark taverns—which he invariably calls saloons—more than bright chain restaurants, and there was a selection of local joints that we frequented for lunch, depending on where exactly the job was. Today, we went to a place called the Indian Head, whose doors Cliff had been walking through for twenty years, and sat down to twenty-two-ounce glasses of beer that were one degree away from being frozen, and oversized burgers and plump fries blanketed with salt and grease. Toby Keith was flowing out of the corner speakers, singing that he wasn't as good as he once was, and Cliff chimed in with, "*but I'm as good once as I ever was.*"

Cliff wasn't the most perceptive guy, and I figured that if I didn't clue him in, he would never guess that there had been any disruptions in my life. He hardly knew how to be any way but jovial, and no matter what mood I was in to begin with, I ended up jovial too after ten or twenty minutes riding in the truck with him. This was partially an act, I knew, because he had assumed a mentor role, and when he'd first rescued me I was habitually morose, so he was teaching me how to appreciate what he called the gift of life. But it was also just who he was—an utterly content blue-collar yahoo who had dialed down his ambitions over the years until minimum effort netted him maximum pleasure. Once upon a time, Mom had told me, her little brother had tried to go to college, with dreams of parlaying his youthful hotrod obsession into an engineering degree, but he had partied his opportunities, as well as his first and second marriages, away. So he had ended up in construction, and then found a niche that caused him limited stress and paid reasonably well.

Drywall, he had informed me on my first day working with him, was so simple that beaners right out of the back of a U-Haul could get the gist of it in a morning, but doing a good job, by old-fashioned standards, was another matter again. "We do it right," he declared, "and that makes a difference. People want beaner quality, they can have it. I don't need their business and they don't deserve my work."

He liked to pretend that he was in a noble profession, and why not? The houses being thrown up at a relentless pace around here were going to have interior walls, and for the time being, human bodies and minds had to get those walls in place, pretty and seamless, so why shouldn't the guy who got it done feel like he was a vital part of the machinery of society? It wasn't like he was just a painter. Those guys, Cliff told me, could have fucking Down syndrome and still get more or less the same results.

Now, sitting at our little lacquered, scarred table in this place that could be lifted right out of 1960—and if you looked at the patrons, right out of *Lord of the Rings*—Cliff leveled his gaze at me and said, "What's wrong with you, boy?"

That was a running joke, of a sort. He liked to call me "boy" on the jobsite, as if I was a black slave, and he addressed me in this way to soften things with a little irony any time he wanted to boss me or demand something of me.

"Wrong with me?" I said. "Nothing much."

"I'm talking wrong with you right *here*," and his gigantic finger floated over the table and pressed into my shoulder.

I said, "Hey!" and shoved his hand away, and felt that knife blade violating the tissue all over again.

He said, "You been squeezing that shoulder of yours all day. Michelle dislocate your arm for you?"

I tried to laugh, and was grateful that I had a touch of a buzz. "You're not that far off," I said, shaking my head, looking away significantly.

"Far off from what? Spill it, boy!"

I looked at him. "She left. She's gone."

Cliff made a face and stared at me. He said, "No! For good?"

"Definitely for good."

"How do you know it's for good?" I could see the joviality leave him, the beer-humor being neutralized. He didn't like this, I knew, because he had taken responsibility for my well-being, and as matters stood, old Uncle Cliff had solved the Kevin problem, stepped up and straightened me around, taught me to work and made it possible for me to secure myself a female. I was no longer a shut-in who thought reality began and ended with glowing screens, and who hardly had the guts to order a coffee at Starbucks. All that had been needed was some old-fashioned fuckin' initiative. Slap that asshole on the back of the head and say, "Let's get going!"

It wasn't like I had to speculate about Cliff thinking this. He had said it all numerous times. Life was simple. You just got busy and things came to you. Everyone wanted to be diagnosed with ADD and depression and all that other happy horseshit, but the one thing they didn't want to do was shut the fuck up and go to work. Of course, when a guy was six-three, and had a voice that carried a mile, and an easy smile and an infectious sense of humor, and had once been a "bronzed god," as Cliff liked to describe his shirtless self, things came a lot easier to him than they did to the rest of us. But after all, Cliff was right, because lackluster me, hardly able to look people in the eye a few years ago, had shut the fuck up, stopped worrying about what might happen, and just gone to work. And, son of a bitch, things had come to me.

Now I said, "I know because I know. She's gone. I wouldn't take her back now if she came begging."

"Aww," Cliff said. "Don't be so sure. Was she fucking around on you?"

I filled my chest with air and looked at him. "Yeah, she was fucking around on me."

"You caught her?" He held his hamburger in two hands, suspended between plate and mouth.

"She confessed. I caught her trying to leave. She had her stuff all packed and was sneaking out, and I caught her and she told me everything." I couldn't bring myself to say the punch line.

"Well, fuck," Cliff said around a mouthful of burger,

shaking his head. I had to wait until he swallowed, and then chased it with a slug of beer. "So what happened?" he said like a swimmer coming up for air. "You tried to stop her and she ripped your arm out of the socket?"

I grunted. "No, I just slipped, messing around under the hood of my truck, and cut my shoulder. I ignored it and it got infected, but—"

"Must be a deep cut if it's bothering you that much. All you gotta do is not let it get infected. Rubbing alcohol, monkey's blood, dishwashing liquid works wonders."

"I know," I said. Home treatment of cuts was a fixation of his. Use whatever tape is handy to stop the bleeding and sterilize the shit out of it. He liked to point out scars on his hands and arms and tell me how they happened and how big and deep they were and how he hadn't wasted time in fuckin' emergency rooms.

"It's fine now," I said. "It just kinda itches."

He nodded, swallowed another bite, waved the topic away, fed himself a fry, wrapped his hand around his damp beer glass. I saw him looking at my wrist, where the fingernail marks were, and I wanted to put my arm under the table. But he just smiled and shook his head a little, like I was a kid with scraped-up knees, like he knew all about guys having their old ladies' fingernail marks on their arms. He sloshed some beer into his mouth and said, "Well, it sounds like that's that. God-damn. After being married and everything. Things ain't what they used to be, I can tell you that. I'm sorry, man. How are you holding up?"

I flashed on Olivia Caruso using the same words, but it wasn't like it was a rare expression. Everyone who has ever gone through any life-crisis has probably heard it from supposedly concerned parties a few hundred times. I said, "Good enough, I guess."

"People get fuckin' married these days like junior-high kids holding hands, then they get in a huff and get a divorce just like that." The two-time divorcé, whose current girlfriend was also twice divorced, snapped his fingers as loud as a firecracker.

"It gets worse," I said. "A lot fucking worse."

"What do you mean?"

"Who she left me for."

"What? Spit it out."

"I mean . . ."

He raised his eyebrows and pushed his moon of a face over the table. He had pale blue eyes and roadmaps of broken blood vessels on his nose and cheeks. His brown-gray hair was sloppy over his ears, thinned to wisps on the large, sun-spotted crown. "Come on, Kev. What is it?"

"She's a dyke now."

"What?"

"She's moving in with some butch lesbian."

Cliff just stared, his mouth open. Some of it was theatrics, but he was, after all, a theatrical personality. He said, "Did you see this lesbian?"

"Oh, yeah. She's a 'friend'"—I made air quotes—"from the college. They've been hanging out for the whole semester. I just never saw it coming."

"God-damn," Cliff said. "Went to college and became a fuckin' lesbian." His eyes went back to his plate, and he soon started eating again, shaking his head and saying,

"Well, shit," a couple of times as his burger and fries disappeared.

We both ate contemplatively for a little while. Toby Keith was back on the sound system, singing "I Love This Bar." Finally, Cliff rapped his knuckles on the table, pointed at me, and said, "You know what the cure for this ill is? You gotta get back on the horse. You gotta get with a real girl. A girl who still likes man-meat. I think I know someone, too."

"No," I said, "I'm not up for it. I need a little time."

"For what? Michelle's a dyke. It's over and done with. She left you. Hell, it's better in a way than if she left you for a man. She's fuckin' loopy. Ain't your fault. So move on."

I shook my head. "It's been like forty-eight hours."

"So set a new record."

"No. I can't."

"Anyway, I gotta ask Mandy. Could be this girl ain't available anymore."

"Who?"

"Mandy's daughter. She's like you—like you used to be. A fuckin' basket case. I shit you not: we were saying a little while ago how it was a shame you were married because you guys are probably made for each other."

Mandy was Cliff's girlfriend. She was in practically the same life situation as he was. I had met her a few times. She was what you would expect if you knew Cliff. A woman just sexy enough for him to want, and just desperate enough to put up with him. A little out of his league in some lights, a bit of a charity case in others. All in all, the arrangement penciled out.

"What's this girl look like?" I said, mostly just playing the part I was supposed to play.

He opened his mouth, caught himself, paused a beat, and said, "I'll show you." He leaned to his left and withdrew his wallet, and from it withdrew a photograph and held it across the table to me, thumb and forefinger pinching the top. It was an obviously old picture of a cute blonde girl with an '80s haircut and a remarkable bust.

I laughed and said, "Sign me up. Where'd we park the time machine?"

Putting the photo back into the wallet compartment, Cliff said, "Well, that's Mandy thirty years ago. Her daughter's twenty-five or thereabouts, so that might be pretty close."

"Yeah, if she doesn't weigh three hundred pounds. You ever meet her?"

"Well, no-o-o," he said, humorously. "If you want to split hairs, I ain't actually seen her. Shit, these days, you might be right. She could be a beluga whale."

"What's her name?"

"Mandy Junior. I don't fuckin' know. I'll ask. I'll have Mandy show me a picture of her."

"I mean," I said, "don't go out of your way. I'm not in the market."

"All right," he said, pushing his plate away, now thinking about leaving. "Shit. A dyke. Michelle went dyke. Who in the fuck woulda thought." He stood and said, "Well, Kev, you still got drywall."

And we went back to work.

10

The first thing I had done after work that Monday was inspect the barn. It was undisturbed. It had drawn no more interest than it had drawn for the last half-century. From anyone but me, at least. That was the day I took my first steps to deal with Michelle and Sabrina. I had no choice in the matter. The unmistakable, vile reek had already begun to seep into the hallway. I had read, probably dozens of times, about how quickly bodies change once life leaves them, but somehow I had not retained, or not quite believed, the information. By Tuesday morning, anyway, I had that situation under control, if not completely resolved.

But by Friday, I was reaching the most distant frontier of my physical endurance. I would skulk over to the barn at dark, after working all day with Cliff, and begin wrenching on the cars. I had imagined that I would break the machines down to heaps of odd components and fenders and tires in a week, but ratcheting nuts and bolts, one swing at a time, and undoing screws with nothing but wrist-power, has limited speed-potential. I began to doubt the wisdom of my plan, but I could imagine no other way to make two entire cars disappear. No other way, at least, that seemed even remotely realistic. I would stop, utterly defeated by the task I had set, and try to think of something else, but the only other conceivable option was a large body of water. I could, I figured, drive the cars one at a time to a lake nearby, but whether I would be discovered doing it, or whether the cars might be found somehow the next day, or even in the next year—and whether the cars might become lodged in mud as I tried to drive them into the depths, or the possibility of some other absurd mishap—caused me to veto the plan each time I began entertaining it.

So I went back to wrenching, and I realized that I was going to have to pace myself. I realized that it might be a month or more before I could start disposing of the cars, piece by piece. I was going to give out physically, and mentally, if I tried to labor every day from nine a.m., when Cliff and I generally hit a job site, until three or four a.m. of the next day, when my body began failing me, refusing to respond correctly to the commands of my brain, no matter how many Rockstars I downed.

On the following Sunday, when the cop knocked on my door, I had begun to catch up on sleep. It was before noon, and I would not make my way to the barn until dark. I heard a car in the drive and peeked through a crack in the blinds and watched the black and white cruiser pull in, and my innards turned to liquid. I immediately went to the bathroom, checked my reflection and finger-combed my hair. The doorbell gave its single *Ding!* I turned off the bathroom light and stepped down the hall.

The cop was a square-faced, tough-looking guy, thirty-five or forty. He had prematurely gray hair, brown eyes that were almost black, and a cage fighter's build under his uniform shirt. The spring sun was flexing, causing me to squint after being in the dim house. His mannequin-smooth face looked more waxed than shaved. His name tag said "P. Kearns." His mouth said, "Hi. Are you Kevin Chapman?"

I said, "I am."

"Do you know what this is about?"

"I think I do."

"Michelle Chapman-Caruso, your wife, has been reported missing by her mother. Her girlfriend, Sabrina Sever"—he betrayed only the slightest twinge of awkwardness at this—"also seems to be missing."

"Yeah, I talked to Michelle's mom—my mother-in-law, I mean."

"So I assume you haven't heard anything."

"No, I haven't heard anything. She left. She doesn't want anything to do with me."

"And when did she leave?" He had taken a notebook and what looked like a mechanical pencil from his breast pocket.

"The Friday before last. I came home, she was all packed up, we had some words, and she left."

He was writing, and did not respond to me. Then he

looked up and said, "What did you guys have words about?" His tone was casual but his eyes were flinty.

"About her leaving me. Pretty much what you'd expect."

He frowned and looked down, pen poised over the pad, and said, "How long did this argument go on?"

"I don't know," I said. "Maybe a half-hour."

He wrote this down, and still not looking up, said, "And then how did she leave? Did her girlfriend get her?"

I managed to feel annoyed at his manner, but I didn't show it. "No," I said. "She hopped in her car and drove off."

He nodded as he continued writing, then looked up again, but not at me. He glanced along the front of the house, then twisted and looked at the trailer. "Who lives there?"

"My mom."

He turned back, locked eyes with me. "Would she know anything about this?"

I paused, as if thinking, and said, "I don't see what she would know. She might have seen Michelle packing stuff in her car or whatever. Maybe she heard Michelle drive off."

He wrote this down, snapped his flat, black-brown irises up to me again and let out his breath as if he'd been holding it. He said, "Okay. It sounds to me like these two young ladies are just off on an adventure, and they need to check in with their families."

"That's what I told Michelle's mom. They could be camping and out of cell phone range or something. I mean, that was last week. I guess they'd be back . . ." I was just talking now, and I regretted it.

My words seemed to trigger a thought in Officer Kearns'

mind. His brow knitted and he said, "How long have you and Michelle been married?"

"Just over a year."

He nodded slowly, and his eyes studied me. I knew, somehow, that he wanted to say something more, something personal, maybe offer his sympathies, but he left it at nodding. "Okay," he said again, "I will get this filed." And then there was a business card in his hand, extended to me, and he said, "You know what to do if you hear anything. That is, if she doesn't turn up, and you hear anything about where she might be."

"Of course," I said, accepting the card.

"I appreciate your time."

"No problem."

And he was walking away, and I was closing the door.

That evening, as I stood in the barn, painstakingly liberating an engine part from Michelle's Toyota—a part whose function I couldn't even guess at—my cell began vibrating. I seldom received calls, but I had contemplated this scenario, and I had no intention of answering while I was in the barn. I would not risk even the distant possibility of anyone, whoever it might be, hearing my voice and becoming alert to the fact that someone had set up shop in here. I wiped my hands on the towel that I had designated a shop rag, and retrieved the cell. The still-lighted screen informed me that I had missed a call from Olivia Caruso.

I had made a crawl-hole on the back corner of the barn, about two feet by two feet, by cutting the bottom off two planks and screwing two more pieces crosswise to them, so they could be used as a door. I had then hung the door with a couple of hinges I had picked out of a flea market bin, and had attached a rusted hasp to the outside and purchased a padlock for it, whose new gleam I had obscured with engine grease. I had screwed both the large sliding door and the man-sized door shut permanently. Nobody could easily enter this place, except by unlocking my padlock and crawling in. Now I crawled out of my secret entrance, set the padlock, and made my way through the weedy nighttime plot, to my house. I retrieved a bud tallboy, drank half of it, cleared my mind, and called my mother-in-law back.

"Kevin," Olivia Caruso answered, sounding grave. "Hello. How are you doing?"

I stared at the shadowed wall. "I'm okay, I guess."

"I know you spoke with a police officer today."

"Yeah, I did."

"He claims he can't help. He is of the belief that Michelle and . . . Sabrina Sever . . . are just being irresponsible."

"Yeah, that's what he said to me. Isn't that the most likely thing?"

"I simply don't believe it. I have never gone this long without speaking with Michelle. Not since she was *born*. A mother knows things. This just feels so wrong."

I remained silent, feeling a tingle of anger. I had been abandoned by my wife, and she was off with her lesbian lover, and now I was supposed to feel something other than satisfaction about her being missing. I wondered how this woman could be so goddamned—

"Kevin?"

"Yes, I'm here."

"I think I'm going to hire a private investigator. That's what the police officer said I could do. Without something more to go on, the authorities' hands are tied. He or she, the private investigator, I mean, will want to interview you, of course, and will want a copy of Michelle's letter."

"Okay," I said. "This is pretty intense." My heart was thumping. I felt a droplet of sweat tickle its way down the small of my back and I reached around and pushed my T-shirt against the spot.

"I'm going to wait just a little while longer. Sabrina Sever's people live in California, I understand. I haven't been able to track them down. I don't know if they have different last names. She and Michelle may be down there."

"I bet that's it."

"I just don't understand why I can't reach either of them."

"I know," I said. "It's really strange. I bet there's a perfectly logical explanation. I'm sorry. I wish I could tell you something."

"Thank you, Kevin. Thank you. I will get to the bottom of this."

"I think everything will turn out fine," I said, cringing at the memory of her saying the same thing to me. Feeling that there was something too obvious about the way the flow of sympathy had reversed direction. She thanked me again, and we ended the call. I finished my beer, my mind now racing. I took another Rockstar from the fridge, and went out the carport door, to cut across the nighttime ground to the barn.

I was thinking now about Sabrina Sever. I had not begun dismantling her Nissan Altima, simply because Michelle's Toyota, teeming with her belongings, had seemed a more pressing problem. I had crammed the accumulated treasures of Michelle's life into black hefty bags, which were now cinched shut and piled in a dark corner of the barn. All of it would eventually have to be burned, I surmised. Every item, every undersized pair of shoes and oversized pair of jeans, every skin treatment and makeup canister, seemed as specific to her as her driver's license.

But Sabrina's Nissan was still undisturbed. It sat where I had placed it, nosed into the barn, crouching on its patch of dirt. I had left the keys in the ignition after I drove it to its final destination.

Now, inside the barn again, I approached the Altima, opened the door, and sat in the driver's seat. There was a rainbow-pattern pine tree suspended from the rearview, lacing the air with a chemically sweet smell. There was a textbook on the passenger's seat. I had ignored it before, but now morbid curiosity compelled me to reach out and tilt its cover up. It was called *Quantitative Analytical Methods in Communication* and was subtitled *Social Justice by the Numbers*. I let myself scoff out a *tshhhh!* sound and flung the book back onto the seat. I then reached over and opened the glove box and pushed my hand inside. I heard myself say, "What in the fuck?" as I realized that the cold, black item I withdrew was a pistol. I had never held a pistol, and despite reading about thousands of pistols in thousands of criminal or heroic hands, I had no idea what type of pistol I held until I read the "9mm" among the information stamped onto the barrel. The handle bore the Beretta insignia. So Sabrina packed a Beretta nine-millimeter around. I quickly saw how to set the safety—which had not been set—and eventually discerned how to release the magazine, which was heavy with bullets. I shoved the magazine back home and felt it lock in place, then sat staring at the thing, weighing it in my hand.

I found myself suffering a fresh attack of anxiety. I looked around the barn, lit by a single clip-on automotive light attached to the raised hood of Michelle's Toyota—and for the moment by the dome-light of the Altima—and imagined, against all reason, that someone was watching me. The discovery of this pistol, it seemed, had broken me out of a prolonged trance. The invisible tethers, connecting my crimes to the outside world, had suddenly become apparent.

I thought then of Sabrina standing over me, and I knew that was at least part of the terror I was feeling: the sudden knowledge of a narrowly avoided, booming, violent death. Why had she not brought her pistol inside with her that morning? Where would I be now if she had brought it? I speculated that she must not own it legally, and she had thought ahead enough to know that using it, or even threatening me with it, could bring her unwanted attention from the police. I remembered Michelle's cryptic statements about Sabrina being some sort of underworld character, and I realized that it was not just a fantasy of mannish toughness. Sabrina was afraid of the police. Sabrina was a real-life criminal.

I found the button that released the trunk latch and stood and walked around to the back of the car. I was envisioning bricks of drugs, white powder packed in clear plastic and bound with brown tape, but the trunk was completely empty. I pulled my phone from my back pocket and activated the flashlight, then reached in and lifted up the false floor that concealed the spare tire, and found the drugs. There were only four sandwich bags, each about a third full of white powder and striped by blue ziplock seals. They sat in the hub of the spare tire. I could only guess what sort of drug this powder represented, but my guess was meth.

I replaced the false floor and closed the trunk lid, not bothering to touch the sandwich bags. I insisted to myself that they meant nothing. I would dispose of them later.

The pistol, though, I would keep.

11

It was a few days later, as we drove to a new job, that Cliff said, “Her name is fuckin’ September.”

I said, “What?”

It was half past eight. We’d had a string of sunny days and this increased the tempo on Cliff’s standard upbeatness. We had just pulled away from the coffee stand, where Cliff spent an extra couple of minutes pretending to flirt with the girls and then gave them two bucks for pretending back. The inside of his truck was a dumping ground for work wares and discarded paper coffee cups and my energy drink cans. He would have an attack of conscience and make it a little neater every month or two, but it ended up like this again by the end of a work week.

As we nosed back into the flow of traffic, he said, “Mandy’s daughter. Her name is September.”

"I've never heard of that one."

"Guess what month she was born."

I made a noise. "I guess you can start calling me May."

Cliff loved to wade into scenarios like this. With his wide smile, and a chuckle in his throat, he said, "Pleased to make your acquaintance, Aunt May, I'm January. January Thirteen."

I did the James Bond bit. Said my name was Twenty, May Twenty, and we went on like this until it started to get lame, and I said, "Well, May is a girl's name. There's June, April. I guess September makes sense. I've just never heard of it."

Cliff said, "Mandy, you know, she's a bit funny sometimes." He raised a flat hand and wobbled it, indicating unsteadiness. "Chakras and auras and all that shit. She says she sensed nine-eleven was coming. She named this girl September Evelyn in nineteen ninety-three."

"That is pretty weird," I said, and did the math and knew this girl was twenty-nine. Michelle had been twenty-five. "Have you seen September?" I asked.

"Yeah, every year."

Laughing again, I said, "Can you imagine this girl's life with a name like that? September Evelyn? What's her last name?"

"Two-Thousand-One. No. I guess it's the same as Mandy's. Rourk. Anyway, here's the good news." He looked at the brake lights on the sedan in front of him and said, "Come on, asshole, wake up. Attaboy. Move it along." Then he said, "The good news is, we're all getting together."

"No shit."

"Dinner at my house, Friday night."

"No shit," I said again.

"None."

"I don't know about that, man." I said. "Two weeks after my marriage breaks up? Really, do you know what she looks like?" I was hoping to beg off on the grounds that she wasn't my type.

We were crawling in slammed-in morning traffic, down a major thoroughfare in Holbrook, the biggest city in this part of the state. I didn't know where we were going. I seldom asked. A job was a job. "Don't be shallow, Kev," Cliff said after a moment. "Your main concern is that she's really sweet. You know the old joke? For every time someone says your blind date is so sweet, you add thirty pounds. If they keep saying what a pretty smile she has, you add sixty."

Laughing, I said, "What are you telling me?"

"She's really sweet, Kev. And she has a pretty smile."

"Shit," I said.

"It's all yours, dude. The buffet's open. You'll know what I mean when you're doing a sixty-nine and you can't hear the radio."

"Come on," I said.

He reached over, rapped his knuckles into my shoulder. I barely felt any pain. He said, "Don't worry, dude, Uncle Cliff wouldn't set you up with a heavyweight champion. Mandy showed me some pictures on Facebook. She's cute."

"Cute?"

"Yeah, she looks normal. Pretty girl. She's got dyed hair or some shit, but I didn't see any major red flags."

"So why is she single at twenty-nine?"

"Who knows? 'Cause she's like you, a fuckin' weirdo.

Maybe you guys have been looking for each other your whole lives. Don't worry about it, dude. See what happens." We had pulled into a residential area and he said, "Is this Dayton Street? Look for five-fifty-two."

Cliff had work thrown at him more or less nonstop, because he knew every other tradesman in the area, and everyone threw everyone else work whenever it came up—at least everyone threw work to everyone else they liked and respected, and Cliff was liked and respected, as far as I could tell, universally. I had heard Cliff tell a client, "I know a guy who can do that, lemme give him a call," about a hundred times, and thus secure a chunk of income for another blue-collar hustler who would return the favor next time the opportunity arose. This time, however, by whatever the process was, Cliff had lined up a regular construction project for us, mostly because the old lady who wanted it done was willing to pay cash. We were to transform the under-portion of a house, which was built on a hill, into a small apartment that the old lady could rent for extra income. After scoping out the job we spent the morning at the lumberyard, figuring out what we needed with on-the-fly calculations, and loading up two-by-tens and pressure treated rim joists and ten sheets of OSB and assorted screws and hardware while the yard guy impatiently lingered and showed us where the appropriate stacks were.

I put September out of my mind until lunch, this time in an Applebee's, where Cliff pulled up Mandy's Facebook page on his oversized phone and thumbed and scrolled for ten minutes, and finally handed me the phone and proved his claim: here was a girl who could not be described as a knock-out, but who could not be described as homely. I couldn't tell what her figure was like in the couple of smiling, fairly chaste mother-and-daughter snapshots. She was, apparently, not overweight. I saw that she had dyed black hair. Cliff tried to tap through to her account, but it wasn't public—or something.

In spite of myself, in spite of everything, I began thinking about this girl, toying with the notion of someone just like me, someone who might actually understand me. I was still thinking about her when I arrived home and saw the guy waiting for me.

Cliff and I hadn't even begun unloading the lumber until the afternoon, and because we were working under a house, we did not realize that it was getting dark, so our stopping point had come an hour later than usual. As I rolled off the street and onto the gravel, the sunlight had almost bled away completely, and I squinted at the grainy form, muttering to myself, *What now?* and *What the fuck?* and other mindless declarations of self pity.

There was no car around. How did he get here? He was sitting on the front step of my house, smoking a cigarette. I thought for a moment of Olivia Caruso's private detective but as I pulled in and got a closer look at him I thought *scumbag*, and then I thought *druggie*, and then I thought of Sabrina's bags of meth and Beretta nine-millimeter. He stood and flicked his cigarette away as my truck settled in. I set the brake and killed the motor, staring at him. He was shaped like a side of beef, thick in the middle. He looked like a Mexican, but somehow bigger, longer, more redneck in his proportions. I muttered one more *What in the fuck?* to myself and opened the truck door and said, "Can I help you with something?"

"I'm looking for my sister."

The blankness, the guilelessness, of his manner, was familiar. I blinked at him, already knowing exactly what was happening, but I asked, "Who's your sister?"

"You know," he said. "Sabrina."

I closed the door of my truck. I said, "Dude, you should just get out of here. How'd you even get here? Where's your car?" I could feel, and hear, the tension drawing my voice thin.

"I took the bus."

It added up like first-grade math. There was a city bus that ran up the county road and stopped across from the Circle K. "How do you know where I live?" I said. "What the fuck do you think I'm gonna do for you?"

"Sabrina wrote down your address. I have it." He patted his front pocket. "I just want to talk to you, bro."

There was nothing comradely in his "bro." I said, "Talk to me about what?"

He looked at me. "Like I said: about Sabrina."

I glanced to the trailer. Mom was home. Had she noticed this person out here? Did she think I knew him?

"So go ahead and talk," I said.

"She told me about the cat. Her girl, Michelle, left the cat here, and there's no way she woulda done that. So something happened to Michelle. And then Sabrina came here and something happened to her. That's what I think."

His intonations were flat, seemingly devoid of both emotion and intelligence. That wild, dark feeling stirred in the pit of my stomach. I said, "You're high, dude. My wife left me for your dyke sister—if she even is your sister. That's all I know. So fuck off."

His posture changed. "Watch your mouth, bro."

"Guy—" I said.

"Don't call me 'guy,'" he cut in.

"Guy," I said again, "get the fuck out of here before I call the cops." I walked toward him, trying to herd him back. I could not get to the door of the house unless he moved. I found myself squaring off with him, and caught a whiff of something putrid—the neglected, seeping, worn-in body-reek of the homeless, or of the person so lost on drugs that he no longer cleans himself. Up close he was big. Not tall, necessarily—although he was about six feet—but *big*. His head seemed to be the size of a five-gallon bucket. His eyes were sunken in, almost completely in shadow in the fading light, so nothing but wet glints showed under the brows. His face was long, and seemed longer due to a tangle of black hair growing off his chin. I had the passing thought that he was an American Indian. Who knew what the fuck anyone was anymore?

"You ain't scaring nobody," he said. "Tell me what's up, bro."

"What's *up?*" I said. "What do you think I did? What could I have done? You're a fucking junkie. You're out of your mind. Get the fuck out of here."

His face twisted into a forced, comically evil smile, and he swung a thumb toward the house. "Well," he said, "I know those girls ain't in there."

I glanced over. The door was closed. "You didn't go into

my house," I said. I knew quite well that I had locked both doors this morning.

"Think what you want," he said. "I ain't got a credit card or nothing."

A credit card? I thought, and then I realized he was referring to ramming the card in along the doorframe as he twisted the knob, forcing the door to unlatch. I had to check now, and I tried to crowd him out of my way and make it to the stoop. I winged the point of my elbow into his chest, and he checkmated me, all at once, with a punch that I never saw. A white flash detonated in my braincase and I was only vaguely aware of my head bouncing off the ground, and only vaguely aware of him trotting away, back to the street, as I fought back up to consciousness.

I got up, my head still swimming, and without waiting for my balance to restore I seized the railing and pulled myself onto the little porch, to the front door. It was, in fact, unlocked. Inside, I thought I smelled his rancid odor. I knew with something like certainty when I saw the empty beer can on the counter. And I knew with absolute certainty when I opened the fridge. I am not above leaving an empty on the counter, but I happen to always be aware of how many beers are remaining in the six-pack, and at last count there had been three, and now there were two.

There was nothing in the house. No remnant of anything that had happened here. Nothing except the Beretta, I realized. I stalked out of the kitchen, down the hall, to the second bedroom. I flung the closet open, dragged my old office chair over, and stepped up onto it. I pushed my hand into the attic opening, which was simply a piece of drywall that rested in a framed hole. I groped, and there was the gun.

I crawled down and collapsed onto the chair. I realized that the gun had to be there, because Sabrina's brother would have had the gun, as he sat outside, if he had discovered it. And then, maybe, he would have recognized the gun, and known everything. Then my mind went to the barn. I quickly worked through the logic, and knew that he could not have imagined, much less investigated, the possibility of anything being concealed in that barn, or he would have attacked me as soon as he saw me—possibly called the police himself.

But I had to wonder if, and when, he would light upon that idea. It seemed that it was just a matter of time.

I was exhausted, but I knew I had to get to work. Sabrina's brother added a new aspect of urgency. He knew. He saw right through my ruse, recognized the truth of the situation with the same eerie, imbecile intuition that had guided his sister. The standards I understood didn't apply with those two. They were, I decided, savages of some kind, throwbacks, ill-adapted to our society of abstract rules and roundabout procedures. They simply saw, decided, and proceeded.

The next morning, at eight, I called Cliff. "I caught a bug," I said. I had never called in sick in almost four years.

"What are you telling me, Kev? We got a shit-ton of work to do."

"I have a fever, I think. I got bad chills. I haven't puked yet, but it's coming. And I got the shits."

"Well, motherfucker," he said, mostly to himself. "Leaving me in a real lurch."

"I'm sorry. I'm sure I'll be better by tomorrow." I lied. "I'd probably get you sick and I wouldn't be much help."

"Eh, we got everything off the truck yesterday. I can wing it today. I just gotta bolt in all the rim joists. Go lay down. Have your mom make you some chicken soup. Be better by tomorrow, all right?"

"I will. Sorry, Uncle."

"Don't sweat it. And hey, don't forget about Friday."

"I know. September."

"That's right. I wanna see you in September, boy."

Laughing, we both ended the call.

I couldn't go to work for two reasons. I had a scuffed, reddened cheek from that punch, and something about my head bouncing off the ground had caused both of my eyes to blacken slightly. I didn't want to explain these things to anyone. In the fridge, along with the two beers, I had some milk, some sandwich stuff that I hoped hadn't spoiled, and three Rockstars. It was Wednesday so Mom had to work at three. I forced myself to rest until I saw Mom's CRV pull out, and then I headed to the barn, to disappear through my crawl-hole.

I was a man possessed. By the small hours of the morning I had made remarkable progress. Both cars were in advanced states of decomposition. The floor was piled with dismembered parts—molded gray metal, black rubber, wires that had been snipped loose wholesale, fenders, windows . . . Anyone looking now would not be able to guess the makes or models. I was over the hump. I decided that I needed cardboard boxes. I would package up everything that was small enough and then stack the boxes along the walls. If anyone was to look in here then, that's all they would see. I would drive over to the shopping center in Holbrook, cruise behind the buildings, and throw a fat bundle into my truck bed.

I had called Cliff at nine that night and told him I was still a wreck. I couldn't keep anything down. He better count me out for the next day. He cursed me, but in a friendly way, and said he was working so well solo that he was thinking about firing me anyway. I asked him if we could reschedule September to Saturday night and he said he'd ask Mandy.

He sent me a text later that said, "On for Saturday. Be there boy."

12

You may be able to imagine the horror that froze me, on Friday night, when I heard a big hand slapping against the side of the barn as I rolled out duct tape across the base of a box which I would soon fill with more automotive detritus. An emotionless, guileless voice followed the slapping, calling out, "Aye, bro. What are you doing in there? Unlock this, bro."

My crawl-hole was catty-corner from where the imbecile was trying to enter, and I snapped off the automotive light and quickly moved to the hole and rolled out of it and set the padlock, before he could wander around to this side. He did not see me as I rounded the barn. My eyes were not yet adjusted to the dark and he was just an ogre-shaped shadow.

He did not jerk with surprise when I said, "What in the fuck are you doing here?"

He just turned to me, almost casually, and said. "I took

the bus. I was looking for you. What're you doing in that barn, growing plants?"

"None of your business, man. You gotta get off of my property."

"I don't gotta do nothing, bro."

"Why are you here?"

"I got kicked out. No rent. Sabrina was handling everything and now I'm fucked."

I realized that, in his broken, primitive mind, his hard luck was my fault. There was something terrifying about it. He was, after all, correct. He was like a dog sniffing its way to something, blindly pressing on, using an instinct that made a mockery of mere logic. Sabrina had been his lifeline, and he sensed her here.

"What do you want me to do for you?" I asked.

"Gimme a beer."

"No. I only have one left."

"Get a glass. Pour me half."

I laughed, feeling as if I had entered the twilight zone. "You can't stay here, man. You have to leave. I'm sorry. Remember fucking punching me?"

"You dug your elbow into my chest, bro."

I had a sudden understanding. I saw that he had simply reacted, answered my violence with greater violence, purely on reflex. Then he had realized that it was the wrong move and run away before I actually did call the cops. I knew, all at once, that the most foolish thing I could do was provoke him.

I took out my phone and thumbed the button. It said "10:18." I said, "You want a beer?"

"Fuckin' aye I want a beer. What did I just say?"

"Let's go have a drink. At a bar."

"Okay."

"Lemme get my keys."

"Go ahead, bro."

His reek filled the cab of my truck as we drove into Holbrook. I asked him what his name was anyway, and he told me it was Isaiah and followed up with nothing. He was content not to talk. It seemed almost as if he was mentally preparing for something. I was content not to risk saying anything that may hit any of his tripwires, so we went along the dark empty roads to town in silence.

When we entered the lighted streets he said, "You know Good Time Charlie's?"

"Yeah, I think. On Central, right?"

"Go there. That's my place."

I said okay and found a parking space a block away from Good Time Charlie's, in the lot of a closed furniture store. We got out, I locked the truck, and we walked up the sidewalk, side by side, like two hit-men on a grim mission.

Good Time Charlie's was right off Main Street in Holbrook, next to a strip club called GQ's. The Friday night scene was just getting into full swing as we stepped inside. The crowd was all under forty. The music laid siege to my braincase, vibrated in my chest. The girls roaming the floor, lingering near the pool tables, leaning over the bar with asses poked out one way and tits the other, were whores. Each one seemed to be advertising her sexuality. I felt a tingle in my loins just breathing the same air as them. I had not thought about sex in weeks. I had only been in this kind of setting a few times in my life, and never as a single man.

The guys were more varied. A lot of cheap wannabe playboys, some androgynous hipsters, a lot of full beards worn as fashion accessories, a few gym-built physiques, a few more in need of gym work.

I did the same thing I saw Cliff do when his boomer taverns were crowded, which was fit myself between two people at the bar with a twenty held up like a calling card, and wait for the bartender to notice. I saw myself in the bar mirror and was pleasantly surprised. It was like seeing yourself on a movie screen. Seeing yourself as a stranger. I had begun wearing my hair a little shaggy this year, because Michelle had once insisted that was the right look for me, and I realized that she was absolutely right. Maybe I did have the good bone structure Mom always said I had. Maybe I was downright handsome. Or maybe bar lighting just has the effect of cosmetic surgery.

Isaiah Sever stood behind me. This was the first time I saw him in any light and for his part, he truly looked like shit. I asked over my shoulder what he wanted and he leaned, scanned the tap handles, and said a pint of Anchor Steam. I got the same. Cliff always tips a buck for each drink. I tipped a buck for each drink, handed Isaiah his pint, and we walked over to an empty spot at an elbow-high counter mounted across the large front window.

I sneaked glances at Isaiah. Even if he had been healthy, his cheeks were pock-marked and sloped down to a narrow jaw, like the face of a cartoon cricket. That face did not seem to match his brown skin and the jet black hair that was like a horse's mane, sprouting densely on his oversized skull in the shape of a haircut that had grown out for a month or two. There was a thin tangle of bristles that he'd let grow long on his chin. In the light, he appeared to be exactly what he smelled like, and what he actually was: a homeless person. He wore a stained gray hoodie, stained and faded jeans, and broken-down blue and white tennis shoes. His skin had a yellow tincture and a waxy layer of sweat and collected grime. It shined gruesomely. When he spoke I saw that he was missing both his front teeth. I thought, *What did you get yourself into, Michelle?*

He drank his beer with big tips of the glass, and between gulps he scanned the barroom as if he was looking for someone.

I said, "This is your place, huh?" We had to speak in raised voices, although the noise was less overpowering in this particular location.

He wiped his mouth with his hoodie sleeve and deigned to angle his black eyes to me. He said, "This is *one* of my places. I own this fucking town." Then he tilted the pint glass all the way up, finishing the drink. He glanced at mine, noting that it was still nearly full.

I started swigging, sensing that it was a good idea not to let Isaiah Sever get antsy. All I really knew was that I meant to leave without him. I had a rough plan of getting him drunk and finding a way to peel off when he was otherwise occupied. This wouldn't keep him from catching the bus to the Circle K and walking to my house again, but it would buy me tonight, and maybe he'd find someone else to latch onto, although I couldn't imagine who.

A short guy walked in, accompanied by two standard-issue twenty-something sluts, one a blonde, one a brunette, who were the same height as him. He looked like a younger, compressed version of the cop, P. Kearns—square face, sandy hair in a fresh fade cut, clean-shaven, probably seen as handsome by girls. He had a tight pastel-red shirt that showed off his wrestler's build. His clothes all looked like they were just purchased. I was surprised to hear Isaiah address him.

"Junior!" the flat, belligerent voice belted out, sounding, as it always did, like a command.

The short guy turned and noted who it was without registering a strong response. He moved toward us while the girls watched him, and managed to sound detached as he half-yelled, "What's up, man." He locked hands with Isaiah in a brief, upright clasp. Isaiah towered over him. He didn't seem to even see me.

As Junior discreetly wiped his hand on his hip, Isaiah said, "I need to talk to you, bro. You know why."

"I'll be here for a while," Junior said, neither friendly nor dismissive. He jutted his chin to Isaiah and said, "Don't forget that twamp."

"Yeah, I know." I saw Isaiah for the first time demonstrate a sort of submissiveness. "I ain't got it now. I'll take care of it."

"Good," Junior said. "I'm gonna get a drink. I'll talk to you later."

I downed the last of my beer and said, "I'm gonna get another. I'll get you one."

Isaiah just nodded. He seemed to be thinking furiously.

When we were on our third beers he decided to open up. He half-yelled, "I ain't gonna rob your plants, bro. People know me. I ain't like that. But if you got extra, I know a dude goes out of state. He'll take everything you got."

I nodded as if I was considering his offer. I said, "Okay. I'm not ready yet." I figured since it was spring, people were growing weed everywhere, and it was natural for a guy like Isaiah to assume that was what I had going on in the barn. Since legalization, I figured the black market would be dead, but what did I know?

I could sense Isaiah's brain laboring. He said. "But that ain't shit, bro. You got that barn there. We can make fuckin' bank. You seen *Breaking Bad?* That's me, bro." He swung his thumb into his sternum. "I can cook. And you got that creek right there? Nobody'll know nothing. We can be rich."

I made a face and nodded. "I'd like to be rich," I said.

Looking across the barroom, he leaned toward me and said, "I don't think you probably did anything to Sabrina or her girl." His words wafted over my face like roadkill carried on a breeze. I frowned and nodded, and felt like laughing in his face, telling him everything. His mind was as easy to read as a child's. He imagined that I was growing pot and was therefore part of his world. He had decided that he had a use for me. He was working up to asking me for money, I knew, to settle his debt and get whatever his fix was from Junior, and he was also fantasizing about me providing him with a source of easy money and easy drugs. The abstraction of his sister, and that whole bewildering situation, lost meaning as he embarked on his mentally handicapped scheme.

I said, "What do you think happened to them?"

He shook his head. "I don't even know, bro. I ain't heard shit. They mighta just took off." He looked at me and smiled, showing the teeth that weren't there. "Sabrina can be a fuckin' cunt, bro. She's only my half-sister. Her mom is whiter than you. I think she got sick of my Indian ass."

"Shit," I said.

"Just like your old lady got sick of you."

"Yeah, I guess so."

"Fuckin' bitches, bro."

"Did Sabrina pack her stuff? Move out?"

"I don't know. I ain't on the fuckin' paperwork. Motherfuckers won't let me back in, even to get my shit. They said I had to get a cop to come with me and that's a joke right there."

"Damn," I said. "That's brutal, man."

"I got good news for you, though, bro."

"You have good news for me?"

"Yeah. That girl right there is eye-fucking you."

I followed his eyes, and saw not a girl, but what appeared to be a woman in her thirties, sitting at one of the raised tables. She had a passably pretty face, red streaks for lips, short dark hair, and a long neck. Her chalk-white legs, naked from mid-thigh in a dark miniskirt, looked like they belonged to a much stouter girl. I imagined that when she stood she would be shaped like a bowling pin. She met my gaze unabashedly, and gave a small wave. Why she singled me out I could not say. I had never been aware that girls were this forward in real life. I had a strange, fleeting conviction that our civilization really is collapsing, just like all the racists and bigots online claim. I smiled politely and gave a single nod.

Isaiah did not attempt to hide his despondency as he said, "You're set up, bro."

"You think so? Just like that?" I felt a quickening. I studied the woman, who was now leaning over the table and talking intently with her overweight, Latina-looking friend, and she suddenly looked to me like the fulfillment of every fantasy I had ever had. I could feel the velvet skin of her neck under my lips, feel where my hands would go. I had to wrench myself out of it. For weeks, I had been on another plane of existence, a plane in which lust was banished by mortal dread and frenzied activity. Now, the spell temporarily broken, the lust returned with whiplash force.

"You been green-lighted."

The woman flashed me another smile, and crooked a finger at me.

"I guess so," I said, swallowing.

"Lemme ask you a favor, bro."

"Okay."

"I need to borrow forty bucks."

"Borrow?"

"I'm good for it. I know where you live."

I barked a laughed before I could catch myself. I was giddy from both the beer and the prospect of sex. The two notions he had expressed were contradictory. He surprised me by opening up his jack-o-lantern smile and saying, "Aaah!" and shoving my shoulder and saying, "You know what I mean." He was on the verge of prying some money loose from me, so he short-wired his sensitivity to insults.

"I don't have forty bucks," I said. "I had to use a card for the last round."

"There's an ATM right there, bro." He pointed to the corner. There was an ATM. I laughed again, and said okay. He smiled for me. I got him forty bucks, slapped him on the shoulder, and went to claim my woman.

As it turned out, I could not follow through. Isaiah disappeared to the back of the bar. I glimpsed him at some point talking to Junior, surrendering my forty bucks, I guessed. I drank and talked with the thirty-something woman, whose name was something that began with a *D*—Delilah, Delaney, I was never clear—but as I talked, I kept forgetting where I was, running scenarios in my mind, flashing on bizarre and gruesome images. Her overweight friend, having become a third wheel, wandered off somewhere, and I pulled a chair next to Delilah or Delaney or Danielle. At one point, I put a hand on her bare thigh, and she took hold of my wrist and encouraged me, and if that had continued that would have been it. But when she went to the restroom, and I found myself sitting alone in this lurid, noisy classroom in Hell University, I could no longer suspend my disbelief, and I just slid off the chair and walked across the floor, out into the night, and managed to drive myself home.

13

The way we humans are made, our egos are always straining against their natural boundaries, and if the pressures of ugly reality let up for five minutes the egos start expanding into new territory, and the next we know we're suffering delusions of grandeur. After one night in a bar, being chosen by one sad slag whose best days were in the rearview, I was having trouble not imagining myself as a stud who could take his pick of sluts in any bar on any weekend.

At dinner the next night, at Cliff's house, I looked at this girl, September, the way a person might look at a car gifted by a grandparent. She was mine for the taking, so I didn't approach like a shopper who was lucky if he could get value for his buck, but stood back and counted up her attributes, debating whether I should flatter her with a claim of ownership. Point One in her favor was her skin, which was not only blemish-free, but of a glasslike smoothness. I would have guessed nineteen before I guessed twenty-nine. Point Two was the deep blue eyes and long lashes, which were undoubtedly her best, or at least most striking, feature. Her hair was bobbed, and not black anymore, but a natural, burnished brunette shade, and I counted her abandonment of the Gothic dye job as a point in her favor. Her figure was a wash. She was skinny, almost boyish, but unmistakably feminine. She had a long, sort of wan face, nothing anyone would call homely, but nothing anyone would rave about.

It was a shame, I thought, that she hadn't inherited her mother's figure. In her mid-fifties Cliff's girlfriend was still built, as Hemingway termed it, with curves like the hull of a racing yacht—however the hell a racing yacht is shaped. If there were strong echoes of Mandy Rourk in her daughter's facial features, there were no reverberations in September's body. That was okay. I'm not one of these guys who is obsessed with obscene proportions. I've got nothing against obscene proportions, but I can consider the whole package.

Cliff, luckily, didn't know how to be awkward, so it wasn't too painful when we all sat down together in the dining room. He made burgers on the barbecue on his deck, and fried his own French fries, and there were Coronas for the men and glasses of wine for the women. Mandy inevitably got around to asking my birthday and informing me that I was a Taurus—which I already knew, although I did not know what it was supposed to mean. She said I was a valiant type and I borrowed some of Cliff's bluster in response, and said well, of course I'm valiant, just look at me, and flexed a bicep. September, she told me, was a Virgo, and was exceedingly practical, and happened to be an excellent counterbalance to the Taurus's willfulness, because we were both Earth signs and saw things in much the same way.

Nobody pretended that this wasn't a setup between September and I. Not much, anyway. An hour in, it was announced that Cliff had only begun with a six-pack, and Mandy's bottle of wine was finished, and why don't you kids—a twenty-nine-year-old and a thirty-three-year-old were "kids" in this scene—go to the McCann's and get another six-pack and another bottle of wine. I made a face at this. I had never known Cliff's garage fridge to not be stockpiled with thirty or forty bottles and cans of three or four varieties of beer. But I played along, and we went, both of us slightly buzzed, to my Ranger, and headed to the supermarket as the sun went down.

When I drunkenly crawled into my truck the previous night I had been horrified at the lingering reek of Isaiah, and had made my way home with both windows down, and when I arrived home I stumbled inside, wet some paper towels, and wiped off the seat cover where he had been. I was now glad I had done that.

Once September and I were in the cab of the truck I cleared my throat, started the motor, and started backing up. The silence was its own presence. I could hear myself breathing like it was it coming out of the speakers. The fact is, if I wasn't imitating Cliff, or if women didn't just advance from introductions to hardcore pornography, I was at sea. I've read about all the scientific pickup methods online, and Cliff has told me that half the girls out there will say yes if you just ask, but I had never tested any of this. When I glanced over at September, her face was blank and she stared straight ahead. So I just drove, and cleared my throat four or five more times.

Finally, as we got rolling on a straightaway, she said, "You're not what you pretend to be, are you?"

I said, "What? What do I pretend to be?"

She said, "Cocky. You act cocky. But you're not at all. It's funny."

"How am I supposed to act?"

"I don't know. Like yourself?"

"Well, this is myself, I guess." I glanced over, and she was wearing a small, knowing smile that annoyed me.

"Yourself is kind of nervous, I think," she said.

"Does that have to do with me being a Taurus?"

"Oh, I don't know about that. That's mom's thing, astrology. I think it's wrong, if you want to know the truth."

"Wrong?"

"It keeps us from seeing what God's plan is for us. It's a way to play God."

"So, wait . . . You're a Christian?"

"Yes, I am." I shot her a glance and she was looking at me with those blue eyes wide open. A challenge.

I had no idea what to say, so I said, "That's cool."

"Is it?"

"Yeah, why not? It's better to believe in something than nothing."

"See?" she said. "Now you're being yourself. You're right. It's better to believe in something. What do you believe in?"

I shot her another glance. "You're not going to try to save me, are you?"

"No, I'm not like that. I'm just making conversation."

"I don't know what I believe in. I guess there's something more than what we experience. I wish I knew what."

"Well, that's a start, Kevin," she said, and then we were at the McCann's, pulling into a slot up front. I might just be a fool, or September might have been a master manipulator, but I started developing feelings for her instantly. When we walked through the supermarket, side by side, I had the idea that we were already a couple. I was acquainted with Lucille, the older woman who rang us up, because she worked with my mom. She looked at me, and then at September, with intense curiosity, but apparently couldn't think of any leading questions. I didn't know if Mom had told her about my marriage breaking up. If so, Lucille must have thought I was quite an operator.

On the drive back, September didn't let silence settle, but instead said, "So . . . your wife."

I was taken with a jolt of sick guilt, not about Michelle, but about misleading September. That's what a fool I am. That's how long it took me to become a sap. I said, "She left me. It was a mistake, getting married. We were only married a year."

"And she left you for a woman?"

"Yep. I guess you know the whole story. It's good gossip. I should have sworn Cliff to secrecy."

"Do you see what kind of world we're in?"

"What do you mean?"

"Do you think that's normal, a wife leaving her husband for a woman?"

"What about a wife leaving her husband for a man? That

happens all the time, doesn't it? That might have been worse for me." The thought then imposed itself that it might have been worse because if a man, and not Sabrina, had come looking for Michelle, he might have gotten the better of me, and I'd be in a prison cell right now. Then I had the thought that Michelle wasn't any rare prize, and no guy would have tried to steal her from me in the first place. That's what it's like in my head. I catch sight of something, and the next I know I've followed it to some place I don't want to be. I realized that September was talking, something about things getting progressively worse . . .

" . . . a hundred years ago," she was saying, "practically nobody got divorced. Men would fool around, maybe. Women never fooled around. Everyone had a mom and a dad and a lot of kids. Then divorce became normal, then marriage became whatever anyone wanted it to be, and now here we are."

"I mean," I said, "I can't really argue against that. Is that why you're a Christian?"

She considered and said, "Something like that."

We pulled back into Cliff's driveway.

I've heard, or maybe just read, that sometimes it's this way. Sometimes you meet someone and it's like you both know, and the bargain is struck instantly, without anyone having to explain. That's how it was with September and I. At nine-thirty it somehow seemed like midnight, like we had done all the visiting possible with Cliff and Mandy, and as the party broke up September and I decided—very casually—that we would go have a couple more drinks or something. Cliff and Mandy managed to suppress their gloating, to pretend as if nothing out of the ordinary was taking place, as we made our way out the front door.

She had driven her little hatchback, and I followed her, valiantly—like a Taurus, I grunted—so if a cop fell in I, and not her, would get the DWI. She led the way downtown, to a place called The Taproom. After my experience of the previous night I was relieved that the music wasn't at nerve-racking levels, and the people were not packed in edgewise and smiling and shouting and slamming down drinks in a state of low-frequency hysteria. We set up at the bar, and both ordered what the bartender recommended, which were pints of some craft beer called Amendment 21. It tasted like beer, but thicker. I said, "So . . . the name September."

"Don't think I don't hate it," she said. "I tried to change it when I was in high school. I used to go by Autumn. But I had known everyone in school my whole life and I was who I was to them. September."

"That sucks," I said.

"It's a real name," she informed me. "There are like five thousand kids cursed with it every year. It just doesn't sound right. And I don't think my mom knew it was a real name when she gave it to me."

"Moms," I said.

"Single moms," she said.

"But where would we be without them?"

She turned the movie-star eyes on me and said, "Where the you-know-what are we with them?"

This had been the source of quite a few wisecracks when we were with her mother and Cliff. As a Christian, she had sworn off swearing.

I said, "Damn. You're pretty hardcore with this stuff."

"I have a right to be. So do you." She looked at me more intently. "I know your life story, more or less."

"Shit," I said. "What do you know?"

She hesitated, and said, "Probably what you wouldn't be proud of, or want me knowing."

I couldn't bring myself to ask for details. I guess she knew she was looking at a guy who had attempted suicide, and still been a virgin at thirty. I said, "Fuckin' Cliff. Excuse my language. I guess he likes to brag about saving me. I mean, he did save me. But that's not all there is to me, you know?" I heard the tinges of a slur in my voice.

"I know," she said, and touched my arm, almost caressed it, and I felt like I could get down and propose to her. She added, "Lucky for me, women are better at keeping secrets."

"What kind of secrets?"

She shook her head. "Uh-uh. Maybe some day."

"Okay . . ."

"Let's just say, this world hasn't been very good to either of us."

"Okay . . ."

She ended up trying to explain her faith to me. She had been converted by, of all things, YouTube videos of C. S. Lewis audio books. I always lit up when anyone mentioned books, and I tried to impress her by immediately naming *The Lion, The Witch and the Wardrobe*, and she didn't quite roll her eyes at that, but waved it away and told me I had to read *Mere Christianity* and *The Abolition of Man* and *The Screwtape Letters*, which I promised I would. I employed a trick I have, which is to reliably record information by relating it to something else. I had "Mere Christianity" well enough. I related "abolition" to "slavery," and "Screwtape" to a mental image of a drywall screw wrapped, for some ridiculous reason, in a piece of duct tape.

I wasn't used to being at a disadvantage whenever the written word, or anything ostensibly intellectual, came up. I tried to steer the subject to my beloved crime novels, or even to Hemingway or Steinbeck or Jack London, and she said, yes, but that stuff is just *fiction.* I made a good defense of fiction, I thought, by pointing out that everyone on the planet knew *The Lion, The Witch and The Wardrobe*, but who knew *The Screwtape Letter* or whatever it was? She told me that just showed how stupid everyone on the planet was. I said that was the opposite of a Christian attitude, and she smiled and said touché.

We left at about midnight. I tried, idiotically, to get her to come home with me, and when she said that was absolutely ruled out I tried to get her to take me home with her. She managed to seem completely sober, and smiled at my ploys, and we entered each other's numbers into our cells, and had a kiss on the sidewalk that I still remember.

I made a last-ditch effort to show off. As she walked to her car I held up a finger and recited, "Mere Christianity, Abolition something, and Screw-Tape Letter."

She said, "Wow, that's pretty good. *The Abolition of Man*, and *The Screwtape* Letters. But I'm impressed. We'll talk real soon, I promise."

And that was it. I was in love.

14

I might have convinced myself that everything was going to fade into the past, and I would have my life back—and maybe even a new and improved version of my life—if it had not been for the private detective. I met Rod Kastrel at a Starbucks in Holbrook. I had suggested we meet there when he insisted that we talk in person. It was the first thing that came into my head. Starbucks are the official, universally recognized landmarks of the modern USA, aren't they? Kastrel didn't exactly insist, I should say. He wasn't exactly a bully about it, but he made clear that he wasn't satisfied with anything said over the phone. Yes, yes, he knew that Michelle was just gone, and he knew that I had no idea where, and there wasn't much more to tell, but he wanted to see if there were any details that I didn't know I knew. It was a thing he did, he said. And it was a lot easier in person. He would get a fuller picture. I thought he was angling to come out to my house, so I headed him off, asked him where he was, and when he said Holbrook I named the Starbucks.

Looking back, I guess he saw through that. I guess he knew that I was trying to keep him from coming to the scene of the crime. That was probably foolish of me anyway, because by now I had the cars stripped to their skeletons, spleens and shed skin, which is to say, to everything but their frames, transmissions, engine blocks, and the separated pieces of the outer panels. The window glass I had broken, using an eight-pound sledgehammer and blankets to stifle the noise. Everything that could be put in a cardboard box had been, and the boxes were now stacked along the wall of the barn. I had dragged or rolled everything to one side, and begun digging a grave right in the barn, about ten feet by ten feet, where the large welded stuff would go. I had it all figured out by now. I would get maybe three feet of dirt on top of it, and make the floor look like it had never been disturbed, and then, some day, I would develop an interest in welding, buy a cutting torch, and dig up and dismantle the rest. In the meantime, I would distribute the smaller pieces somehow, pitch them into a body of water, or maybe take them to the dump, a box or two at a time, along with other junk, when I took a notion to remodel the kitchen or something.

On the phone, Kastrel sounded like he could be in broadcasting. He had a deep, rolling voice, and he was practiced at using it. He said the perfect things in the perfect way. He was almost hypnotic. In person, he was fat. The kind of fat where it makes your mind reel, because it seems like it can only be the result of the grossest negligence, or even a personal mission of achieving and maintaining a ball shape, and you can't figure out why someone whose mind seems so keen, and who speaks so nicely and precisely, would not be able to manage his physical self. And it gets stranger, because Kastrel, when he finally stood, after our interview was over, was also quite short. No more than five-four. Standing before him, I felt like an Earthling encountering some waddling alien species that was compressed down by the heightened gravity of its home planet.

He had tipped me off, in a way, by saying, "Look for a fat guy with a beard." I walked in, and there at one of the tables for two was a fat guy with a beard—maybe fifty, maybe sixty—looking right at me, and we both knew who the other was as soon as we made eye contact. Another thing about guys that fat is, it can be hard to tell their age, because the wrinkles that fold over and collect on a normal person's face get filled in and spread out.

And here's another layer of strangeness: If you just considered his face, Kastrel was a handsome guy. His beard still had color, and it was trimmed close, like a professor's, and sliced off neatly at the bottom so it gave the illusion of a jawline. He had a sort of sculpted, hawk nose, a square forehead, and his gray hair was combed back from an un-eroded hairline. If you only had a picture of his head, and only heard his voice, you would think this was someone particularly favored by God.

He was already working on a sixteen-ounce something—I've never bothered to learn the Starbucks lingo—and when I said I could use a cup he said, "Please, go ahead, I'm in no hurry," and he picked up his phone and was, or appeared to be, instantly transfixed by whatever was on the screen. When I sat down across from him with my twelve-ounce black coffee he looked up with a pleasant, distracted expression, and thumbed the side of his phone and set it, face-up, on the table.

"First, nice to meet you in person." He extended his hand over the table. "I'm Rod Kastrel, as you know, and I've been hired to find Michelle Caruso-Chapman, your wife."

I shook his hand and just said, "Hi, good to meet you." I found myself wondering if his phone was recording us.

"This is nothing formal or official. I go on instinct, mostly, and I want to get a feel for what might have happened to Michelle and, apparently, her girlfriend."

I just nodded. Something about his smoothness made me distinctly un-smooth. And I was thinking about his phone recording us. I wondered if the girlfriend reference was meant to rattle me, or if that was just what it did, every time, however it was meant.

"So, Kevin, what do you think happened?"

"I mean," I said, "I don't know. I have no way of knowing. I came home from work, Michelle was all packed up, we argued for a while, and then she took off."

"Was it a bad argument?"

"Not the worst argument we've ever had because she wouldn't, you know, engage with me. She was over me, acting like she felt sorry for me. So I finally just had to let her go." I had worked out my story since talking to the cop.

"I see. So you guys argued for what? A half-hour?"

"Yeah, probably that."

"And Sabrina Sever. Did you talk to her?"

"After that? No. She wasn't there when I came home from work. And then Michelle left."

"What do you know about her?"

I thought about Isaiah Sever. I couldn't bring myself to mention him. I said, "Just that she's kind of a lowlife."

"A lowlife?"

"That's the impression I got. Michelle talked about her before they were . . . a couple. And she kind of hinted that, like, basically, Sabrina sells drugs and roughs people up when they don't pay. She thought that Sabrina was a badass. I mean that was the impression I got."

He nodded and said, "Well, that's certainly interesting," and he seemed to be studying me. Then he said, "Do *you* have that impression of Sabrina?"

I frowned, thought a moment, and said, "She looked—looks—like she wants people to think that about her. That was what I thought when I met her." I knew I had made a mistake by using past tense. I had read this in enough fucking crime books. Some guilty fool starts talking about someone who is only missing as if they're already dead. Kastrel might not have noticed, but I fixed that by correcting myself. I thought of making an excuse, saying well, I know they've been missing so I've started thinking of them as being gone for good, but I knew an excuse would just sound like an excuse.

"What kind of look is it that Sabrina has exactly?" he said, too smoothly.

"Like a man, basically," I said. "You know, she's a butch lesbian. She has short hair, and wears, like, work clothes."

"So just her clothes?"

"Her clothes, and her act. She tries to talk like a man, walk like a man, and she gives people hard looks, doesn't say much."

"I see. So do you think Sabrina being a lowlife has anything to with her and Michelle going missing?" There was no challenge in his manner. He was doing a beautiful impression of someone who was on my side, collaborating with me to get to the bottom of this.

I said, "I have no idea. No idea at all. Michelle left me a note, and said they were moving away, her and Sabrina, and I guess they could have just taken off. I don't know why Michelle wouldn't call her mom."

"Ah, the note," he said. "Mrs. Caruso mentioned that. I'd like to have a look at it."

"I don't have it here, but you're welcome to see it. I can give you a copy."

"That would be fantastic," he said, then a perfectly timed pause, and then, "Well, Kevin, you've been very helpful." He picked up his phone and deposited it in a side pocket. I muttered something and he stood, and I had the shock of only seeing him unfold to a little higher than I was sitting. "I will come by and pick up that letter," he said. "I can make a copy and leave the original with you, or if you have a scanner you can make a copy. Is it handwritten?"

"No, it was typed on her laptop and printed."

"I see," he nodded. "Well, that's fine. Thank you again," and he put out his little square hand. We shook, and I stood and made my way out while he waddled toward the restroom.

15

"Hey, Kev?" my mom said when I answered her call the next afternoon. "Are you in some kind of trouble?"

A frigid wind seemed to blow through my body, freeze-dry my guts. I felt nothing but a sense of unreality for a moment, and then it was all too real and my hands became unsteady, my nerves on high alert. I was covered in mud and sweat, standing under an overcast sky on this deceptively warm day, digging a ditch that ran from under the old lady's house, out to where it would connect with the four-inch line that ran to the city sewer. I managed to say, "What are you talking about?"

"This little fat fucker is here," she said. "He's a private detective he says? He was grilling me about you and Michelle. He seemed really nice. I thought he was worried about you, but now I'm not sure. He asked if he could take a look around the property, and I should have told him no, but I couldn't think of any reason to stop him. I thought he was trying to do you a favor. Now he's traipsing all over the place."

"Mom," I said, "that guy's . . . not cool. I don't know what he's up to. Michelle's mom hired him. You can't let him just go nosing around on our property."

"So I should tell him to leave?"

"Yes!" I said. Did she not understand what I had just explained? "*Tell him to leave.* Don't tell him *I* told you to tell him. Just tell him you changed your mind, because it's weird to have him poking around."

"Yeah, okay, I'll run him off."

"But be polite about it."

"I will. The fucker has some nerve on him. He acts like butter wouldn't melt in his mouth and then starts looking in windows like a peeping tom."

"Where is he now?"

"I can see him right by your house. He was over by the old tractor barn before."

"Tell him," I said.

"Yeah, I'm telling him."

She hadn't terminated the call, and I heard her as she moved to the door of the trailer and opened it, and said, "Hey, mister?" and then the call ended.

Cliff, who was digging a hole where the main sewer line was supposed to be, said, "Something wrong with your mom?"

"Oh, no. Some guy was on our property and she thought I knew him."

"Sounded serious," he said.

"No, it's not. The guy took off. You know your sister. Fuckin' drama queen."

"Yeah, I know my god-damned sister," he said absently, bending back into his hole. He did not like to lose momentum when a job was underway.

I put the phone into my back pocket again and took hold of my shovel handle, which I had leaned against my stomach. I flung another shovelful of dirt onto the pile on the tarp beside the ditch, and felt barely able to stab the shovel-point into the dirt again. I knew it was over, and I saw how crazy the whole thing was, saw that it was always going to come to this, and I almost felt relief. But at the same time I began combing over the details, looking for a glimmer of hope.

I knew that he could not get into the barn. He might *know*, but he could not have seen anything that would remove all doubt. Even if he saw my crawl-hole, which he would have to wade through branches to find, he would only learn of the existence of a small, padlocked door that it was probably physically impossible for his girth to pass through, even if he had the gumption, or some kind of tool—or the strength—to pry the hasp loose. The big sliding door, and the man-sized door, were fastened shut with planks of wood and dozens of screws. He would have better luck tearing them apart than trying to open them. And I had coated the barn's interior with tarpaper so thoroughly that he would not be able to peek inside—and even if he tore a hole in the tarpaper somewhere, he would see nothing, because the interior of the place was pitch black if the clip-on automotive light was not turned on. The one thing he would probably see, that I could not hide, was the first in the chain of extension cords that delivered electricity to the barn. The one that was visible was dark green, and it poked up randomly from the dirt and ran across the corner of the pavement, where it was plugged into an exterior outlet in the carport.

"Keep up!" Cliff said, and I realized that I had stopped working.

"This is the worst," I said. "I'm not used to working outdoors, you know."

"Eh, you're thinking about your new favorite month."

"No, I just can't match your old-man strength."

"You know what they say," Cliff said. "The bigger the nigger the better the digger."

Mom appeared very shortly after I entered the house that evening. Daylight savings had bumped sunset back an hour, so I wouldn't be able to sneak over to the barn for a while yet. I answered the door, and she came inside, and followed me to the kitchen.

"It sure is quiet over here now, isn't it?"

"Yeah," I said. I had already thought, and I knew she was thinking, about her moving into the house and having me take the trailer. I had no intention of agreeing to this, and I hoped she didn't bring it up. I looked at her and I had to keep myself from scowling. Sometimes, like after you've been talking to someone like September, you see people through new eyes. The daylight was not kind to Mom's sixty-four-year-old face. With her fake-youthful body and fake-healthy hair and fake C-cups she looked like Haggard Skank Barbie.

I got a beer out of the fridge and cracked it. I could feel her eyes on me. She said, "Honey? Can you tell me what's going on?"

"Nothing is going on, Mom," I said, turning, resting my hip against the counter. "You know everything I know."

"This little fat guy? This private detective? He's really got me worried. He wanted, like, every detail, especially of the night Michelle left."

"Good. I'm glad you told him. I don't have anything to hide."

"You never told me who she left you for, Kevin."

I said, "Am I supposed to brag about that? It happened. Michelle is a fucking dyke now. What do you want me to say?"

I had an impulse to throw my full beer against the wall. Mom's syrupy sympathy had a way of bringing out the worst in me. I was forever the five-year-old who had skinned his knee, and the more she laid it on, the more of a sullen brat I became. She never cared about the five-year-old, she just wanted him to quiet down. Now she wanted me to quiet down her fear that this situation was going to cause her any sort of inconvenience.

"Honey?" She was blinking at me now, intent. "You didn't do anything crazy, did you?"

"No, mom. I didn't strangle Michelle and her dyke lover and then hack them up into little pieces and bury them in the yard. What do you think?"

She seemed relived when I put it this way. She said, "Okay, okay. I don't know. It's just so weird, those two . . . girls . . . just vanished."

"Mom, they're adults. Michelle left me a note saying that she was moving away. The only thing that has everyone freaking out is they haven't called home. I don't know why. Maybe someone did kill them. This Sabrina girl, she was a real lowlife. She sold drugs."

Mom's eyes flared wide and she said, "*Was*, Kevin?"

"Fuck. *Was. Is.* Whatever. If they're dead somewhere then it's *was*. I was talking about the possibility of them being dead. That's what I was saying."

"Okay, okay," she said again. But she was looking at me in a peculiar way and I suddenly remembered how easily she could become my enemy in this. If she thought I was guilty of the worst, would she risk anything to protect me? Would she turn me in to protect herself? Would she revel in the drama of it?

"Mom, listen. I've been kind of a wreck, you know? You have to cut me some slack. I never saw this coming. I've just been getting by, trying to keep my cool. Then Michelle's mom starts calling me, telling me she hasn't heard from Michelle. I don't know what to make of that. And now this private detective guy wants to drag me into that situation. It's a nightmare."

"You say this girl, this lesbian, is a drug dealer?"

"Yeah, that's what I heard."

"I bet that explains it. You see this stuff in the news every day. Except it doesn't stay on the news. Nobody thinks it's gonna come all the way into their own lives, and then it does. It used to be that nothing like that was ever heard about in these parts. Was that her who came here, the night Michelle left?"

"What?"

"The person who came here after Michelle left? I saw someone pull in, Mark and I, as we were leaving."

"Did you tell that to the detective—to Kastrel?"

"Yeah . . . shouldn't I have?"

"No, I mean, yeah. It's fine. I had food delivered. But he's going to think it means something. That's probably why he wanted to go poking around."

"You had food delivered?"

"Yeah, Mom. I never do. But I was starving after work, and there was no food in the house, and I didn't want to go anywhere because of the situation. People have food delivered all the time." I raised my eyebrows and looked hard at her. "Stop!" I said, feeling my voice thicken. "Stop suspecting me of this shit, okay? You're making everything way worse." I felt the sting in my eyes and blinked. It was like a chemical reaction that Mom caused in me. I never melted down with anyone else.

Mom said, "Oh, honey," and stepped up and started rubbing my arm. She was back to soothing the five-year-old. "I'm so sorry this is happening. It'll all be in the past before you know it."

Now I was sniffling, the world around me blurred, and I said, "I hope so," and we hugged, and her fake tits were like two cantaloupes pressing into my stomach.

16

I still don't know if Rod Kastrel was a master of psychological warfare, or if he was just certain, in his own mind, of what had happened to Michelle and Sabrina, and was afraid of meeting the same fate. Whatever it was, when he came to pick up the note, he brought muscle. This was pretty much exactly twenty-four hours after my conference with Mom in the kitchen. I watched through the window of the second bedroom as they got out of Kastrel's new white SUV. If you've seen that old movie *Twins*, with Danny DeVito and Arnold Schwarzenegger, you have a pretty good idea of what met my eyes. The guy who got out of the passenger's side rose up over the top of the car, and his physique was that of a competitive bodybuilder. He wore a casual, navy blue, short-sleeved dress shirt, but there was no concealing the chest and shoulders, or the knotted lumps and webs of veins that enwrapped his lower arms. He looked to be a mulatto, or something not quite mulatto. His buzz-cut head was round as a tennis ball, and his nose was wide and his lips oversized, but his skin was light and freckled. As he rose out of the passenger's side, Kastrel labored out of the driver's side, something not quite a dwarf, but walking a little like one as he moved all that extra weight.

I met them at the door. I tried to keep my face blank.

In his oily pitchman's voice, Kastrel said, "Hello again, Kevin," and extended his hand. As we shook he said, "This is Mason Smith. He's in sort of an apprenticeship program with me. Try not to get us confused."

We all chuckled. Mason Smith and I looked at each other and he said, "Hi, Kevin," and bent a little, reaching around Kastrel, and gave my hand a quick clasp. His handshake was unaggressive. He had no need to demonstrate his strength, and seemed to want to put my mind at ease about it. He was, it seemed, working to imitate Kastrel's disarming manner. He did not look quite as big up close. Only about six-four. Only about two-eighty.

"I have the note right here," I said, turning to where I had placed it on the coffee table.

"Do you mind if we come in and talk to you for a few minutes?" Kastrel said, blurting it slightly.

I opened my mouth, nothing came for a moment, but I finally said, "Well, I was just working on something . . ."

"Just five minutes."

He had fed me a line when he called, told me that he had the address and happened to be driving through Brunswick yesterday, and decided, on a whim, to see if I was home. He said Mom was very sweet, and he was sorry if he'd overstepped his bounds playing Sherlock Holmes. He laughed at himself. Just a clown pretending to be a great detective. I wasn't rude to him, but I left his explanation sitting there, just said, "Uh-huh."

"Sure," I now said, stepping back. "Come in."

The living room was nicer than any living room that I was in charge of had a right to be. That first summer, when everything was a dream, Michelle had hunted up the furniture, and had put up a couple of artsy framed pictures. We had a vast flat-screen mounted into the wall studs, opposite the front window. There was a couch from Big Lots and an armchair from a yard sale and a coffee table from the St. Vincent DePaul's. It all worked together and made a nice layout. Everything was a bit dusty, though. I had spent no time in here since the night it happened. When Kastrel and Mason Smith sat on the couch, Mason immediately had a sneezing attack and I went in the kitchen and got him a paper towel. He used it noisily, folded it, and put it in the breast pocket of his shirt.

Kastrel smiled with only his lips. I sat in the armchair. Mason apologized for disrupting the proceedings.

"Very quickly," Kastrel said. "Your mother told me that someone else was here the night Michelle . . ." he considered and said, "moved out. That wouldn't have been Sabrina Sever, would it?"

"Uh, no," I said. "I ordered food. I had it delivered."

He nodded and said, "I see. That makes sense. If it ever came up, if it was necessary, we could find where you ordered from, credit card records, all that. So I guess that's good for you." He gave me a smile.

I worked to keep my face blank. Mason Smith shifted and sniffed and pulled on his flat nose with thumb and forefinger. Kastrel was on the edge of the couch, his stump legs holding him up, his globe torso bisected comically by the waist of his pants.

"And then, yesterday," he continued, "I happened to notice the old barn there," he indicated the barn with a lean of his head. "People will give you good money for that wood, you know. Picture frames, siding, some people even use it for flooring."

"I never thought of that," I said. "There are old barns all over the place around here."

He held up his palms, shrugged slightly. "It's a thing, barn wood. I've thought about redoing my den with it. Maybe I'll make you an offer on some of that wood from your barn."

I stared at him and said, "Yeah," in an idiotic way.

"That barn over there is buttoned up awfully tight," he said, looking into my eyes.

"Yeah," I said.

"Can I ask why?"

"I mean," I said, "I don't really want to say."

We looked at each other. I looked at Mason Smith. He had an expression of intense interest. His eyes were a shade of brown trying very hard to become yellow.

"It's not like it's illegal. I just don't want my mom to know," I said. "I don't want a big thing made of it."

He seemed to realize what I was getting at. "You're . . ."

"Growing," I said, making the word significant. "You know, growing. 'Hemp.' I'm making side money. That doesn't have anything to do with this." I waved a hand as if our situation was a thing that occupied physical space, in the general location of the thrift-store coffee table.

"That explains the little path worn between here and there, and the power cord, I guess." He smiled with genuine friendliness now—which made him handsome, which made him surreal.

"I thought I had that cord pretty well hidden," I said. "I don't want my mom knowing."

"You guys have separate power bills, of course."

"Yeah, we do."

He took it all in for a moment, nodding, then said, "And the note?"

"It's right there." I pointed at the coffee table, which had nothing on it except the sheet of paper.

Kastrel rolled forward, an exertion for him, and extended a stumpy arm and gathered the note. He produced a pair of bifocals from a breast pocket and set them on his nose, then held the letter at just the right distance and read it quickly. In the silence his labored, nasal breathing became embarrassing. I could not imagine how someone so shrewd and gifted could allow himself to become what he was. He lowered the letter, removed his glasses, and said, "That seems to explain it, it doesn't it? I think Mrs. Caruso will get some comfort from seeing this."

"I hope so."

Then, with a few muted grunts, he stood and began waddling to the door with the weightlifter moving behind, haltingly, like a car stuck in traffic.

Before he exited, Kastrel took hold of the doorjamb and

turned to me and said, "Where did you order food from, anyway?"

"I don't even remember," I said.

"You don't remember?"

"I drank, like, a whole bottle of whiskey after Michelle left. I wouldn't have remembered that I even ordered food if my mom hadn't mentioned seeing someone here."

He looked at me like he'd never heard anything that stupid in his life, but he said nothing. He just thanked me again and made his way out.

In the barn, as the night tipped over from the p.m. to a.m. hours, I had finally reached the plateau. The miracle had taken place. Everything that could not be unscrewed or unbolted, reduced to something I could lift with my two arms or fold or break or compact, was beneath a few feet of dirt. A web of tree roots had sought to prevent the digging of the automotive grave, and many of the subterranean tendrils were as big as my arm, but Grandma and Grandpa had bequeathed Mom and me some ancient garden tools, among which was a dull axe and the shovel that had facilitated this and other burials. So I had worked through the impediments, and thrown the severed root pieces in on top of the metal, before I shoveled the dirt back into the grave, compressing it with boot-stomps as I went, and scattering the excess around the floor when I was done.

The floor was now empty, and stacked three-high along the back wall were the cardboard boxes, some white, most the natural tan, some fresh-looking, some with stains of various automotive fluids darkening them. The main supplies of motor oil and gasoline had been drained into a five-gallon bucket, and then poured into the creek, which still ran six or eight feet wide at this time of year.

The tarpaper that lined the interior of the barn absorbed the light, and the space was cavernous, weirdly lonesome, and suddenly, unaccountably, terrifying. I stood staring, and panic began to mount. I was convinced for a fleeting moment that ghosts were in here with me, and then I was certain that something had been overlooked—and then that everything had been overlooked. It was all too obvious, and Kastrel already knew, and soon everyone would know. I should have come clean from the beginning. I had the knife wound. I could claim self-defense. Instead, I had been dismantling my future. Digging my own grave.

I stepped back until the wall stopped me, and then I lowered down until my ass was in the dirt, and bowed my head into my hands. I knew I had to dig myself out. I described to myself how it had happened, and why it had happened. I blew on that ember of hatred, of defiance, until a flame sprang up, and then I kept thinking, and the fire grew.

I raised my head, opened my eyes, spread my hands, and looked down at them. They had become brutal things in this short period. Thickened, torn and scarred, with maps of swollen, blue-green veins overlaying their backs, snaking down the tops of my fingers. Those hands seemed to belong to someone else, and then they seemed to belong to an alien race. I thought: *Why do we humans even exist?* Here I was looking at the same hands that my ancestors, stretching back a thousand—hell, ten thousand—years, had looked at. Wasn't it the same skin, the same bones, literally reincarnated? The spongy pulp inside my skull, the stuff causing me to have these very thoughts, and this face and whole body, for that matter, were what those ancestors had given me, what they had fought, and fucked, to maintain and pass along. Here I was, the same exact person as some soldier or cobbler in England or Germany or Scotland from ten or twenty centuries ago, flung out in this distant land, in a dystopia of cell phones and single moms and insane lesbian wives. And I had no offspring. This was the end of all their struggles. I thought: *Maybe this is Hell. Maybe I am them, in Hell.*

And with that thought, I was liberated. What does it all add up to, anyway? Everything was already lost. Everything had been lost from the day I was born. From the day the first asshole in my particular line had been called Chapman. So fuck it all. I might as well go down fighting.

I let my hands droop, turned my head, and contemplated the boxes.

The goddamn barn had to be empty.

17

I discovered I was being watched when I was on a date with September that Friday. A six-four skeleton carrying a hundred-fifty pounds of iron muscle can provide a lot of advantages, but inconspicuousness isn't one of them. If he was not built on such a large scale, the black baseball cap and loose black hoodie might have allowed Mason Smith to blend into the scenery, and from enough of a distance, or when he was sitting down, they had that effect. But when the guy stood up, the people around him were just a little too small, and whether you had met him before, your eyes tended to find him in a crowded room. And once you were looking at him, if you had seen the smooth, round, not-quite-Negro face up close and at length just a couple of days before, it was likely that your cross-referencing equipment would come up with a match, and you would know with a sudden, disturbing jolt, just who you were looking at.

We were in an Irish pub in Holbrook. Kilkenny's was not a crass hookup den and drug marketplace for the local millennials and early zoomers; it was a pub-slash-restaurant with ancient brick walls decorated with antique artifacts and framed pictures from better eras, and waiters and waitresses in green polo shirts with shamrocks on the breasts. A couple of scruffy guys plunked out theoretically authentic Irish music and sang through their noses on a little stage up front, and it wasn't so loud that you felt you were trying to have a friendly conversation in the middle of a hurricane. There were other couples on dates, a collection of regulars and lone wolves languishing along the bar, and a few teenagers and even one or two little kids eating with their parents at tables, since it was still early.

The date had been a remarkable success until I had noticed Smith. September was several steps up for me. She wore a sleeveless shirt and a long skirt, and had done some kind of magic with makeup and blurred her short dark hair with a blow-dryer or something, and my initial impression of a physically bland and slightly sad young woman was swept away. This girl was in all respects of a higher caliber than Michelle had ever been, and that made her the most attractive girl I had ever had anything like a romance with. Being with her in this setting gave me the novel experience of feeling that I was just as good as anyone else.

But, at the risk of getting the eye-roll, the best part was the conversation. You have these conversations online sometimes, and you scroll threads and read a lot of other people having them, but all of that ends up like half-remembered dreams. In real life, when you have no friends except a guy like Cliff, and when your wife, however she might pretend, has a strictly pedestrian intellect, you start wondering if you're insane for thinking about things other than the endless sewage-flow of politics and the latest celebrity crisis. Sitting face-to-face with a flesh-and-blood human, and especially a girl who looks better the more you look at her, and being asked to consider whether this reality is a simulation, and whether we all exist in the mind of God, was a drug I never knew existed. I found myself becoming downright eloquent, working like hell to impress September and having breakthrough after breakthrough. And that was an even more exhilarating drug.

And then, I found myself blinking over her elegant, bare shoulder, seeing that massive dark shape, and then looking away from that wide-nosed face, and then looking back at it as my blood became liquid nitrogen. He had no idea I was looking at him, because he carefully avoided any tilt of head or shift of eye that might suggest awareness of me, and I stared with all my might as he went toward the back of the building, as a rectangle of daylight appeared, and as he went outside. Kilkenny's happens to be cavernous, occupying a two-level store space in one of downtown Holbrook's aged commercial buildings, and there were about fifty yards, and fifty people, separating Smith from me. If he was someone else, he could have safely assumed that he was camouflaged in the hubbub of the room, but the guy was too big.

"Hello?" September said, waving a hand in front of my

eyes. "Did something from another plane of existence actually materialize?" She turned and looked over her shoulder and then looked back at me.

I grinned emptily. I felt the haze of the strong beer. He was gone now either way. I said, "Sorry. I saw someone. Someone my wife is friends with, and I thought she was looking at me. I don't know if she was, but it weirded me out for a minute."

"Your wife," she said, opening up the topic. "That sounds so serious."

"I mean," I said, "it is in a way. Or you think it is. I was serious."

"And then she left you for a woman."

There was something about her manner that was, if not bitchy, then territorial. I didn't entirely dislike it. I sensed my leverage in the situation. She didn't want me to have any lingering interest in Michelle. I had a brief glimmer of *If only she knew,* but I was smart enough to play coy. "Yeah," I said. "Like we were saying. This modern world is chewing people up and spitting them out. Michelle is a victim."

"Unless we have free will," she said, picking up a thread from our previous discussion.

I was lured back in. "How can someone who is taught that black is white, and day is night, have free will?"

"How can someone seriously believe that black is white and day is night?"

"So you think moral knowledge is innate?"

"Yes, I do."

"What about, like, Muslims, or Indians—I mean, you know, Native Americans, way back when—people who think that honor killing, or pitching gays off roofs, all that kind of stuff, is moral."

She stared at me, processing. She said, "They are guided by sound moral knowledge. It's primitive, they may go about it wrong, but it's not like they're pretending that black is white and day is night. They're not lying about basic reality. That's when you misuse your free will. When you lie to yourself, try to reverse some inconvenient truth for the sake of your ego."

"And Jesus, he says . . . "

"He tells you to think very hard about how you put your moral knowledge into practice. That's the next level. Jesus assumes you aren't going to lie about basic reality any more than Muslims or primitive tribes would lie about it, and he's telling you to ask yourself what's really right, instead of just, you know, *acting.* Jesus is telling you not to be primitive."

"Jesus," I said, leaning back, accidentally making a pun and then pretending it was deliberate.

"That is the answer," she said.

"You really don't seem like a Christian," I said, "except when you talk like that. I mean, I don't know. Maybe I've only seen caricatures in the media."

She smiled her row of pretty teeth and I sunk another inch into the quicksand of infatuation. "I'll take that as a compliment," she said. "I'm not a Bible-thumper. I don't watch televangelists or anything. I don't even have a regular church, I'm sorry to say. I think a lot of those caricatures are true. That's kind of the challenge."

"How do you mean?"

"You have to read your Clive Staples Lewis, my friend."

"Okay, but explain it to me."

"What if something is true, but it's considered, like, an embarrassment to believe it? And it takes a lot of personal humbling, self-effacing, to get to where you can even try to believe it, and you have to deal with all these freaks who say they believe, but who aren't that bright, and are just on their own types of ego trips?"

"So Jesus made Christianity toxic, as a test?"

"No, Satan made it toxic. Jesus just challenges you to proceed in spite of Satan's tricks."

"Jesus," I said.

"That is the answer."

I had no idea what to do on an actual date, and especially with a Christian. We weren't going to binge-drink in any old bar we happened to end up in, and then drive drunk to one of our places and have sex, and spend the next day dazedly nursing hangovers, going out to eat, wearing silly smiles and making stupid jokes. That had been maybe seventy percent of my courtship of Michelle. The other thirty percent was going to the movies, and I suggested that option to September, but she said that anything they're going to put in theaters, even kids' movies, are "literally Satanic," so that was out.

She did smile when she said "literally Satanic." She was aware of being a cliché, and that made her much less of a cliché. But I still found myself wondering what all this could be leading up to. Either this girl was nuts or the entire world was.

I also found myself wondering if being seen with September, by these people who suspected me of a double homicide, cemented my guilt to them. Unless you knew the story it was natural to assume that I had wanted Michelle out of the way, and now, within just a couple of weeks of her disappearing, I was openly dating this slimmer, prettier thing that I obviously—they would think—had waiting in the wings. This worry was augmented by my growing awareness that I was not a preordained loser in this life—that I was, as everything averaged out, attractive to women. If only someone besides Mom would have explained this to me fifteen or twenty years ago. But what my animal magnetism, if that's what it was, meant to Kastrel and his sidekick, was that I was likely to have been cheating on Michelle, and that had a lot of implications in a situation like this, didn't it?

We ended up walking around downtown as it became dark, and September took hold of my arm, and I wished she hadn't, and she sensed it and sort of casually let her hands fall away, and I said, "Sorry, I'm not used to, you know, public displays of affection. Michelle and I weren't hand-holders or any of that. It makes me self-conscious."

"Maybe that's why she started dating women," September said.

I was too shocked to be offended. I laughed as I said, "Now *that*—that is definitely not a Christian thing to say."

"Oh, it could be," she said.

"How do you know I'm not sensitive about the topic? Is it Christian to mock something I'm already ashamed of?"

"How do you know I'm not sensitive about taking your arm and then getting snubbed?"

"I'm not a Christian," I said. "It's not immoral for me to be inconsiderate."

"It's still immoral. You're just letting yourself off the hook. That's why people should be Christians."

"Jesus," I said. "You really play hardball." And I stopped walking, lifted my elbow like a gentleman in an old movie, and said, "Please. Sorry. I don't mind. I'll get used to it."

She looked at me for a moment, and then she said, "No, thanks. Maybe another time."

"Jesus," I said.

She said nothing in response. Just the understated smirk.

As the sky took on the final glassy emptiness of dusk we walked into the old park in the middle of Holbrook. It boasted a Civil War cannon and a couple of gallant statues, a pretty antique pavilion in its center, and a community of homeless junkies on the eastern patch of grass, lurking among their heaped shopping carts like a bunch of raccoons. Some new law had made the city homeless-friendly, so these old-fashioned hobo jungles—with the modern twist of decriminalized hard drugs and self-important and often downright menacing bums—had appeared in any patch that looked inviting. If there happened to be a grassy island between two lanes of traffic, there would be a shopping cart piled with debris, and its owner either doing a shift with his cardboard sign or, if you looked for a minute, you'd notice him right there on the ground, wrapped up in two or three sleeping bags, getting his eight hours.

I had been making excursions into Holbrook for my entire life and I could remember when people were, if not boastful about it, at least not ashamed of it. It was the biggest little city in the valley. It still had tatters of its mid-century heyday—and of America's heyday—clinging to it everywhere you looked. There was the downtown area with its dignified elderly buildings, the dead art-deco movie theater, and the Woolworth building on Main, letting you know that this was once a regular Mayberry, USA. There were the blocks of nice-looking craftsman-style houses sprawling around downtown, the structures now bleached colorless and settling back into the earth, occupied by welfare cases. There were even some blocks of embarrassed Victorians from the very early days, set back behind grand lawns, some still kept clean and freshly painted. But now, unless you counted the row of giant chain stores that had been erected along the highway, the town was dying, actively decomposing, and its pretenses of normalcy were pathetic, like a smelly old dog with arthritis and mange hanging out its tongue and beating its tail.

We found an enthusiastically run ice-cream shop that would be closed by next year, and got a couple of scoops and small cups of coffee for desert, and then wandered some more, and wound up getting cocktails in a low-key retro place because our imaginations failed us. I finally got to the topic of my crime books, and told her how Hemingway broke trail, and how Hammett, Chandler, and Cain then established colonies, and how Thompson and Goodis elevated the genre to art. I told her how noir holds the bad guy sympathetic, and hard-boiled features bad guys who are really good guys, but how modern detective fiction is just romance novels for men. I either impressed her or made myself look like a freak, but she seemed to become interested, and to have some kind of realization as I spoke. I seemed to have scored a point with all that, finally.

At the end of the night, which came at only eleven, we had an old-fashioned make-out session in the shadows next to her car. I guess it was what I had missed out on in my high school years. Her hands patrolled mine, gently clasping wrists and keeping things from going to the next level, and I accepted the boundaries she set—her Christian values—and we parted ways in a state of romantic intoxication. I waited until she had the doors of her hatchback locked and the motor warming up, and walked back to my truck, hands in my pockets to hide my exuberance.

18

The following morning, when I saw the familiar number on the lighted screen of my phone, I wasn't surprised. I had been anticipating this moment, and I nodded my head and said aloud, "Here we go," and thumbed the icon and lifted the device to my head.

"Hello?"

"Hi, Kevin," the DJ voice said. "It's Rod Kastrel. Could you spare me a few minutes this afternoon?"

"Sure, I guess."

"Would the same Starbucks as before work for you?"

I was relieved that he didn't want to come to the house again. I said, "Yeah, I can do that."

"Make it one o'clock?" he said.

"Sure."

"Excellent, excellent. Thank you. I'll see you then."

"See you then."

The call ended.

I stood in the kitchen, staring at the phone in my hand, and inventoried the situation. If the actual police showed up with a search warrant, I supposed I was finished. The barn was now empty, and I had pulled down the tarpaper on a wild impulse, because it seemed to scream guilt. But there were about two thousand staples sunk into the redwood in there that I intended to pluck out with pliers, but had not yet gotten to. And I had visited the dump to dispose of the tarpaper, and a few other items, and there were records of that, I had to assume, and maybe even security camera footage. And if they took a metal detector into the barn they would find the car frames and engine blocks and transmissions. They may even discover—although I couldn't imagine how—what was in a few deep holes, in various locations along the creek, far enough from the bank so winter floods could not dislodge them. But that wouldn't be necessary if they got into the attic and found all the boxes of car parts lining the far sides of the roof structure. And I would certainly have some explaining to do if they came across Sabrina's Beretta.

I parked at the Starbucks in a slight daze. The day was bright, the sky clear. The place was buzzing with activity, the drive-through line extending into the parking lot. I was showered but not shaved, because I had shaved the previous evening before my date, and my jaw only had a barely visible sandpaper growth. I wore jeans and a plaid flannel shirt, which happened to have a cigarette burn-hole on the front. I had bought the shirt at the Goodwill last year, because it was apparently brand new and it was my style—which is really no style at all—and had not even noticed the hole until Michelle pointed it out. It was still one of my favorite shirts, but I now found myself agonizing about whether something could be read into that burn hole.

I went inside. The Saturday Starbucks crowd was casual, mostly middle-class men and middle-aged ladies seeking their caffeine fixes, playing at being sophisticated. A homeless guy sat in the corner with his backpack between his ankles, looking indignant. A couple of perky twenty-something girls, one white, one Hispanic, and a tall handsome obvious homosexual worked behind the counter, the homosexual wearing a headset. I scanned the room and there was Kastrel, once again already at a table, this time a four-seater, already drinking his coffee. I guessed he always showed up ten minutes early.

This time, I declined to get myself a coffee, and just scraped the blond wooden chair out and sat down. We shook hands over the table again and said our hellos and pretended that he didn't suspect me and that I didn't suspect him of suspecting me. He proceeded to affect the good-natured confusion that I had read about in so many crime novels, but unlike those classic detectives, his act involved his cell phone, which had notes that he was frowning at. "Now," he said as his eyes lifted and held mine, "I just need you to help make a couple of things square up for me. You say you're growing, er, hemp in that barn. When did you start growing?"

"I . . . haven't started. I was going to. I was working with a guy who knew all about it, but he flaked on me, so that plan is canceled."

"So, you had the barn buttoned up so tight because you were planning on growing. But now you're not planning on growing."

"That's right."

"Could you give me the name of the guy you were going to work with on that?"

"I'd rather not. He would probably be upset with me."

"Just in case," Kastrel said.

"I shouldn't. I . . . can't."

He nodded as if making a notation to himself. He looked at his phone and scrolled down with the tip of a sausage finger. "Okay. And you say you ordered food on the night Michelle and Sabrina disappeared. That is, apparently disappeared." He looked up, his eyes bland, his voice innocent. "Now, your mom told me it was a dark car, black or gray. And Sabrina Sever happens to own a gun-metallic-gray 2018 Nissan Altima."

"Yeah, well," I said. "I see what you're implying, but—"

He shook his head. "Oh, no. Please. I'm not implying anything. I'm just making you aware of what might be implied, so you can make it make sense. You've seen the shows. You know that if the police decide to press the matter, you will be put through the wringer. My job at this phase is to figure out if the police should be brought in. To either locate these young ladies or determine what might have become of them. That's why Mrs. Caruso hired me. So, this is really easy for you, relatively speaking. You just have to deal with a nice little fat guy. As long as everything adds up." He smiled.

I gave him back a smile that was supposed to reflect his friendly act, but that felt queasy. I said, "Okay."

"Did you order food through an app on your phone?"

"I don't—I mean, no. I know I didn't because I don't have any of those apps on my phone."

"So you called some place, and ordered food, and they delivered. You would have had to give them a credit card number, right?"

"I don't remember. I might have paid cash when they got there."

"Does anywhere do that? Deliver food without securing payment first?"

I made a face, shook my head, raised my hands. *I don't know anything about anything, motherfucker.*

"You understand how this might look. A car that you can't prove was not Sabrina Sever's was at your house. And your barn is all battened down like Fort Knox for a reason you can't, or won't, prove is true." His eyes changed, and he raised a finger. I realized that a call was coming in on his cell, which was set to vibrate. He jabbed the screen and put the device to his head and said, "What's up?" He listened, V'd his brows, and said, "Really . . . *Really* . . . Oh, excellent. Tell you what. Know the Starbucks on Dover? Can you bring him here? I'm with Mr. Chapman right now. Let's all put our heads together . . . Excellent . . . Right." He took the phone away from his head, terminated the call, and set the phone back in front of him.

I purely hated the sound of that conversation. I just knew that this fat fuck was dealing from the bottom of the deck. His eyes twinkled at me. "There's another thread we've been pulling, Kevin, without much success until now. Sabrina Sever has a brother. A pretty rough character. We've had a hell of a time locating him, but Mason—you remember Mason—is with him now, and he's going to try to bring him here."

"Oh." I felt my system kicking over into fight-or-flight. My blood started to sing in my ears. I didn't know if I could talk properly.

"Are you okay?" Kastrel said.

"No—I mean *yes*. I'm fine."

"On the other matter," he said, "I just had a thought. You should have the phone-call to the restaurant logged on your phone. This will be very easy to put to rest. Do you have your phone with you?"

My mind raced ahead. I said, "No, it's in my truck. Actually, I think I left it at home. I'm pretty absent-minded a lot of the time." I could feel the blood broiling the skin of my neck from within, and I hoped he couldn't see it starting to glow red.

Kastrel sighed, not trying to hide what he was thinking. "That's too bad. We could most likely just stop bothering you if we could verify that."

I sighed and looked out the window. If only I had known, I would have called some fucking restaurant that night and then hung up. By what an idiotic thought—

"Do you know Sabrina Sever's brother?" He asked.

"Um, no, I don't think I do," I said.

"You don't *think* you do?"

"I mean . . ." I was drawing a blank. I could, I thought, excuse myself for a trip to the restroom, and then just walk out the door, get in my truck and leave. But then what? They knew where I lived. I glared out the window, watching people in the parking lot, and then I was watching Mason Smith, Mr. Universe himself, with black biker shades wrapped around his tan tennis-ball head, resting on his sideways question-mark nostrils. He was back in his short-sleeved dress shirt, standing out of the driver's side of a dark SUV. Isaiah Sever, not quite as tall but probably the same weight, got out of the passenger's side. He looked like he'd had a shower. His untrimmed, coarse hair was combed backward from his forehead. The tangle of greasy hairs hung off his chin, but his jaws looked smooth. His barrel body was in a checked flannel, half a size too small, probably appropriated from a Goodwill bin. His expression was his standard belligerent vacancy.

Kastrel followed my gaze and said, "There they are."

"Yeah, I know him," I said.

"Well," Kastrel said, and now the two massive men were inside, moving toward us, both looking at me looking at them.

Isaiah gave me a chin-thrust. I had the sudden sense that he was here against his will. I said, "Hey," in response to his acknowledgement, and then I looked at the lenses of Smith's black shades and gave a nod. He nodded back. A single head-bob. We were, so damned conveniently, at a table with four chairs, and I now found myself with Isaiah Sever's bulk settling in beside me, crowding me without touching me, while Mason Smith sat beside Kastrel. Isaiah's stench was diminished, but apparent. I was surprised when he put out a hand for an upright clasp, and I put my palm to his briefly. He said, “Aye, bro. I ain’t forgot that twenty.”

“Uh, yeah,” I said, fleetingly noting that he had halved the amount owed me. That was his version of conning me.

“So how do you two know each other?” Kastrel said.

“My sister’s girl,” Isaiah said. “That’s his wife. Like I told this guy here,” he chin-pointed to Smith.

It came to me from nowhere. “This is the guy,” I said to Kastrel. “We were going to make side money.”

“Aye, man,” Isaiah said, “what are you—”

“Growing,” I said to him. “And the other stuff . . . In the barn at my place. They know about that.”

Isaiah visibly stiffened. I saw the storm start swirling in his brain. I had an impulse to get clear of him. His face smoothed, became even more expressionless. He threw a belligerent chin-thrust toward Mason Smith. “You setting me up, bro, or what?” He turned to me. “Is this a set-up, fucker?”

“No, man,” I said, leaning away, holding the edge of the table. “I wouldn’t do that.”

His hand slapped the tabletop and he said, “My sister, motherfuckers!” addressing us all. “That’s what I’m here about.” A lady with an empty-wallet face and a swept-over brown hairdo gave us an annoyed look from the next table.

“That’s what we’re all here about, your sister,” Kastrel said, a hand up. *Nothing to get to excited about.*

“You motherfuckers actually cops?” Isaiah said. “You telling me stories, but you’re cops?” His hands, brown as if permanently filthy and flecked with white scars, twitched on the tabletop.

"We aren't cops," Kastrel said.

"I knew you was bullshitting me. I ain't here to talk about no fucking barn. Show me your fuckin' badges, motherfuckers."

"We aren't cops, Isaiah," Kastrel soothed. Mason Smith was now half off his chair.

"Then fuck you, I'm out," Isaiah said, and slid from under the table and stood, and now he and Mason Smith were both standing, facing each other. Smith still had his shades on. Isaiah's head was tilted up to face the taller man, cocked sideways, like he had one bad eye. The Starbucks noise seemed to have funneled away to nothing but nervous muttering and a euphoric female vocalist, accompanied by electronic jazz, leaking out of the ceiling speakers. A scrawny young guy, tattooed from his wrists to his cheeks under a black T-shirt, had begun capturing it all with his phone, standing and circling just out of range, hoping for something upload-worthy.

"Just have a seat," Mason Smith said, looking robotic, cool. Then he put his hand on Isaiah's shoulder, his forearm bunching as the fingers closed. At this, Isaiah seemed to hesitate, to question himself, just before I saw the same punch that put me down whip from his hip and send Smith staggering. The giant man crashed into a knot of people milling where the orders came out. He caught himself against the counter, just managing not to fall. Starbucks filled with gasps, Isaiah was already scrambling, and people were drawing back. He made the door, heaved through it, and went running across the parking lot.

Mason Smith recovered, took off his now-crooked sunglasses, and went darting for the door with bugged eyes, looking like a bona fide action hero. I heard him say, "Look out, excuse me," in an almost-polite voice, to a couple of people starting to step into his path. He made it outside and went running in a professional sprint across the parking lot, in the direction Isaiah had gone.

Five minutes later, except for the surreptitious glances being sent our way, Starbucks had returned to normal activity. The lady with the empty-wallet face had asked if she should call the police and Kastrel said no, thank you. Mason Smith had his shades on the table, and a reddened and swollen upper lip. Isaiah had successfully vanished, and Smith's failure to catch the guy seemed to have shaken him to the foundation of his being.

Kastrel had sweat beads on his forehead and red splotches on his cheeks, but his voice was congenial. He said, "Well, now we know something. I'm not sure what. Do you want to elaborate on that situation, Kevin?"

"I mean," I said, "it's pretty much what you heard. We were going to, you know, grow weed. He said it was legal, and he could get the lights and stuff on spec, so it wouldn't cost me anything, and we could make like twenty grand when we harvested it. I had the barn right there, and I could use the money. But then he wanted to set up a meth lab, like in *Breaking Bad*. He said he was the best cook in the valley and we could make ten times as much, but that was too sketchy for me, so I backed out."

Kastrel was studying me. Smith seemed to be somewhere else.

"When did this start?" Kastrel said.

"I don't know. A few months ago. He came over with his sister once, before I knew that she and my wife were, you know . . . " I moved my hands to complete the thought. I said, "He kind of scoped the place out, and then, when we were alone, he got me to agree to it. Sabrina was in on it. I mean, that's what I think. They worked together. It was like Sabrina came over, saw where we lived, and then they hatched the plan."

Kastrel was nodding, but his eyes were hard.

Smith said, "I wish I had caught that fucker. That's our man. Hundred percent."

"Maybe, maybe," Kastrel said, and his eyes and then his head turned, slowly, toward the bigger man. He might as well have called Smith an idiot out loud.

"Are you going to get the police on him?" I asked.

"We just might," Kastrel said. "I need to talk to Mrs. Caruso. There are still some things that don't add up."

"Oh yeah," I said. "I was thinking: it might have been him who showed up with food that night. He might have been driving his sister's car. I just had the boxes there in the morning, so I thought I must have ordered something. I was blacked out."

Kastrel stared at me, doing all he could to figure me out. I held my face blank. After a few seconds he said, "I see. What kind of food was it?"

"Chinese."

He pondered this with his eyes lasering into mine. He was, I knew, scanning for inconsistencies, trying to beat my checkmate. He apparently couldn't because, finally, he just gave a slow nod.

The meeting finally broke up. Kastrel wanted to be rid of me for the moment, it seemed. He wanted to pick everything apart, go over it with Smith.

As I drove home, not even seeing the prettiest day of the year so far, I had no idea where this left me. I could only think about Isaiah Sever. He seemed to hold my fate in his hands. I wondered if he was getting out of town. On a level that I didn't yet understand, I hoped that he wasn't.

19

It was late afternoon. I was too close to the edge, repeatedly trying to sigh away the tension, feeling my system ready to spiral up into a cleansing rage. We were at a park in Brunswick that consisted of little more than a picnic table, four swings on their A-frame, and an industrial playground set built in the updated fashion, made of thick yellow, red and black plastic. Winter was a memory now, and the world was an oil painting, all plant life vivid and burgeoning and the sky some pure blue squeezed right out of a tube. The playground was being used by three Mexican kids, tromping and sliding and squealing and bickering incessantly in Spanish, with the momma and poppa standing by together, interacting with the kids in Spanish from time to time. Cliff had a lot to say about tripping over goddamned Mexicans everywhere you went anymore even in this goddamned state, and it was hard not to see things his way once it got into your head. The parents looked to be about twenty-five, as uniform in their features, hues, and builds as animals from the same den. The woman, I saw, was pregnant. I wondered if they wondered what was wrong with the fully-mature gringo couple sitting at the picnic table. Where the hell were our kids? I wondered if they had the idea that they were just waiting the Americanos out. Keep breeding, don't make waves, fast-forward twenty years, when all the gringos have died off or become elderly, and you own the place. If I was them, that's what I would be thinking.

But the main thing on my mind was that it was probably over for September and I. The seal of the little world of just we two had been broken. We were suddenly just a couple more fools standing naked in a wasteland.

She had said that we needed to talk, and it couldn't wait. She had mentioned, like, maybe, a park? and I had suggested this one, and now I was convinced that she didn't really think it was too pretty not to be outside, that she wanted to meet somewhere where she could run for it or scream for help.

"I guess you should just tell me," I said.

She nodded. "This guy," she said, "this giant guy, came up to my car after you left on Friday."

I felt nothing. In that moment when the bomb is whistling down but it hasn't impacted yet, you feel nothing. I said, "Yeah? And?"

She glanced toward the playground, at the Mexican parents. "He told me that you're a suspect in a murder investigation." She spoke too quickly, her habitual coolness showing cracks.

"He lied," I said. "There is no murder investigation. I talked to the police already. My wife, she's missing—"

"Why didn't you tell me that?" Her voice was just slightly shrill. Her remarkable eyes wide.

"Because." I glanced at the Mexicans and dialed down my voice. "Because if I told you that these private detectives were, like, stalking me, and what they're accusing me of, that would be it, right? You wouldn't want anything to do with me. So what am I supposed to do? Listen, Michelle left me a note, saying that she and her *girlfriend* were leaving the area. And then she's gone, with all her stuff. So I figure that's the end of it. But her mom can't reach her, and she hired this guy—not the guy you talked to, but his boss or whatever, a little fat guy named Kastrel—to find her. And that guy is all over me, I guess because he doesn't know where else to start."

"But weren't you the last one to see her? To see *them*?"

"No!" I went back to the well. "No. The thing is, my wife's girlfriend," I sighed. "My wife's girlfriend was—*is* a lowlife, and she's got this brother who's a total druggie . . ."

A little of the fear-wattage went out of her eyes. She was hearing me.

"The brother," I said. "He was the last one to see them. He was driving his sister's car. He came over to my house."

"Why would he come to your house?"

I sighed. "Because I have this old barn there. It's kind of embarrassing. Kind of sleazy. He wanted to use the barn to grow weed, and I was going to go along with that, make extra money, but then he wanted to set up a meth lab, and I backed out. And when I did, he attacked me." I was coming to believe my own story. I wished I had mentioned to Kastrel and Smith that Isaiah had decked me.

"He attacked you?"

"Yeah, he lost it and punched me out—sucker-punched me—and then ran for it. He wasn't driving that time. He took the bus out there for some reason. He no longer had his sister's car. And when I told him we couldn't use the barn he freaked out on me. Right in front of my house. So, that's all I know about it." I felt my eyebrows cranked all the way up my forehead. The very picture of flabbergasted innocence. "I mean, there's this lunatic, strung out on whatever—meth, heroin. The guy is not all there. He's pretty fucking scary. Sorry, but he's a total freak. If they're really missing, if something really happened to the young lovers, it obviously traces back to him."

I told her the story of the Starbucks, what had happened to the very same guy who had spoken to her, and I could feel her coming back across the divide, stepping onto firm ground with me again.

"It comes down to the police," she said. "These detective guys can think whatever they want, but if they've got nothing, if nobody presses charges, then they're just spinning their wheels."

"You're right." I nodded, again struck by this streak of distinctly un-Christian pragmatism. Was she saying that, guilty or not, all that mattered was whether I was busted? I felt the need to emphasize: "And there's nothing to make the police think it's me, and there's the druggie who's the obvious culprit."

"It's a mess," she said. "But it's not the way I thought. It's just a mess."

"So you don't think I'm a crazed killer?"

She looked at me, and the smirk had crept back. "Probably not. You just have a little baggage. And as baggage goes, yours isn't the worst."

I said, "uh . . ." and she fixed those eyes on me.

"Why don't you take me out to dinner," she said, "since we're already here together?"

"Okay."

We went to Don Felipe's, the nicest of the three Mexican restaurants in Brunswick. The place was perpetually, as Cliff put it, "like Grand Central Station at train time," and this evening was no exception, but the booths with high-backed wooden benches afforded privacy, and the wait staff wasn't required to call you "amigo" like at the second-nicest place (the third nicest was just the taco-truck business model, but inside a should-be-condemned building). We got Coronas and she teased me for "inhaling" the basket of chips. I ordered a burrito grande, she ordered a taco salad. Mine was to be methodically devoured. Hers was to be prodded with a fork and, occasionally, tasted. But I had been wrestling lumber, crawling on top of wall-frames all day, fixing ceiling joists in place. She had been trimming hair at the Family Cuts. When my burrito was about half gone she said, "Okay, are you ready for a confession?"

We looked at each other. The moment took on significance, as she meant it to. I said, "Maybe. I don't know."

"Remember how I told you that I became a Christian by watching YouTube videos of C. S. Lewis audiobooks?"

"Yes, I remember that."

"That wasn't exactly a lie? But it wasn't the whole truth."

"Okay . . . "

"I mean, I did really get it, once I started listening. But I *read* C. S. Lewis first."

"I'm appalled," I said. I put my fork down. "I'm leaving. I never imagined you were that kind of person. Reading—"

But she was looking at me too intently. "*Mere Christianity* was given to me," she said, "by a fellow inmate."

I said, "By a . . ." and then I said. "Ah . . ."

She was looking at me so hard that I had to lean back. Her pupils were dilated, her eyes more magnetic than ever.

"You were in prison," I said.

"For three years."

"For what?"

"Big picture? Drugs. Specifically, armed robbery."

My hand had abandoned my fork on the plate. I wished the guy would come and offer another beer. "You—what? Knocked over a bank?"

"A Quick Stop."

"By yourself?"

"No, with my boyfriend at the time. He's still locked up. I was an accomplice."

"Jesus," I said.

"So," she said. "I guess I have a past."

"You could say that." I stared at her. Where were the trashy tattoos, or the knife scar down her cheek? Where was the tough speech and low thoughts? I said, "September, the hardened ex-con," and smiled, not just out of politeness.

"First it was September the insecure adolescent, trying to

get attention in the world of Mandy, the aging party girl, with the rotating cast of young boyfriends. Then it was September the junior party girl, learning every wrong thing I could possibly learn. Then, along the way, it became September with her own real boyfriend, except he was not just some player who wanted what guys wanted from Mom, because I don't have what Mom has. Mine had to have a dark side. Mine helped me graduate from liquor and pot to coke and meth."

"And then armed robbery," I said.

"No, that wasn't him, actually."

"Oh."

"I was an addict. I ended up pretty far down the food chain."

I nodded, slowly. I said, "Man," a couple of times. Then I asked, "When did you get out?" immediately regretting the clichéd bluntness of the question.

"Two years and three months ago. I've been pretty much a shut-in since then. No real friends. Definitely no dates. I didn't even drink anything for a year and a half. I read, exercised, completed cosmetology school—beauty school—and watched YouTube videos. Then I had a glass of wine with Mom and it was no big deal. So now I have a drink, occasionally, socially. Drinking was never my problem. I just never drink alone, never keep anything in the fridge."

"Jesus had no problem with wine."

"This is true."

"You seem so . . . above it all. I mean, to have that—to have been in prison."

"I am above it all now. I'm trying to be." She was studying

every nuance of my face, looking to see if I was disengaging, trying to figure out if she had just killed our relationship in its crib. I knew why she had done it, though. She felt like she had been lying to me, proceeding under false pretenses, and her Christian conscience was troubling her. And then she realized that I was a bit seedy, after all, and she got an impulse.

I smiled, let out a breath, and said, "We're a couple of salvage jobs, I guess."

I could feel her relax a little. She said, "That is one way to put it."

I said, "Oh, yeah, our souls. I didn't mean that. Your soul is saved, maybe. I don't think mine is."

"I'm not totally sure about mine, either."

I didn't like the insecure version of September. I said, "I'm not bothered by all that. By your past. It's ancient history. I'm not exactly living a storybook life myself." I reached out and opened my hand in a vacant spot on the formica tabletop. She placed her hand in mine, and I folded my fingers around it. I saw that her eyes were glassy and her cheeks flushed. She blinked, and a tear broke free and rolled down her cheek, and I thought, *What in the fuck am I doing?*

20

I don't know if Mason Smith was acting on his own, or if Kastrel had told him to find out what was in the barn. Unless he had a metal detector, however, he was out of luck there. It looked the way it had looked for the past fifty years. I had backed out all the screws from the interior, and removed the planks from the man-sized door, so he just had to push it open. He had used his cell phone light, and filmed all around, I was to learn. But I had plucked out most of the staples, and removed the hinges and the hasp from the crawl-hole, and attached the makeshift door to the rest of the planking with black drywall screws, which became invisible in the dense shadows that defined the inside of the structure.

It was three days later, in the evening after work, that I heard the whir of a car motor, and the crunch and pop of gravel, and looked out the window to see the black SUV with Smith's round head and oversized shoulders floating behind the steering wheel. My mouth was suddenly dry. I went to the kitchen and freed a tallboy from its ring. I cracked it and had the bottom tilted toward a high point on the wall when the doorbell gave its single *Ding*. I took the beer with me to the front door, opened it, and looked up at Smith, who was looking down at me with a strange intentness. I said, "Hey." We had been wiring the old lady's soon-to-be apartment today, so I wasn't too dirty or too exhausted.

Smith's tongue wet his turned-out lips. I could not read his thoughts. "You, Mr. Chapman," he said, "are a lucky motherfucker."

"Really," I said.

"But your luck is gonna run out. Let me just give you the word. We know, me and Rod Kastrel, we know. We got your lying ass cold."

"Really."

"Really. But maybe you know the law. Maybe that's why you're so lucky. The cops ain't gonna move on it with what we got now."

"The cops?"

"Oh, that sticks in your craw, don't it? They know. They know how your story is a pile of bullshit. Ordered fuckin' food. Nobody's seen hide nor hair of these girls since *you* last saw them."

"I told you, Isaiah Sever—"

"That guy," he said. "You know what I think? I think we find that guy, it's over for you. I think he knows shit he don't know he knows. That's what I think. I think that barn—" he

tossed his head to his right—"has some stories to tell. That's not what I think. That's what I *know*."

I could now hear, when he spoke at length, the jolty, bastard-Southern, African-American intonations in his voice. I wondered how he picked those speech patterns up in this part of the world. Was it genetic? Probably, I decided, it was hip-hop or Hollywood. Life imitating art.

"So, then, what?" I said. "Why are you here?" I felt myself slipping, getting that dark wild impulse. I imagined something bad happening to this fucking monster.

"Because Rod Kastrel is out."

"Out?"

"That's right. You're gonna think you won the lottery. The man had a heart attack. He's out."

"Dead?"

"Good as. But I ain't dropping this motherfucker. I know—I *know*—that those girls never left this place. Maybe it was you and Sever, but I just don't think so. That piece of shit told me he came here looking for his sister."

"He's not right in the head," I said.

"I think you're not right in the head."

"Yeah? How do you think I made them and their goddamned cars disappear?" The words made perfect sense as I was taken with the impulse to speak, and then I wanted to rewind life and bolt my mouth shut.

I could almost hear the *click* in his mind, and his eyes sharpened. I thought, *Fuck*.

Smith said, "That's the million-dollar question. That's where that barn comes into play."

"Go ahead and look in the fucking barn!" I blurted.

He grunted and twisted his face into a lips-only smile. He said, "I already looked, son." He lifted the cell phone that was already in his hand. "I filmed every inch of that place. I was here for a fuckin' hour today. You don't like it? You think I broke the law? Call the cops on me. I fuckin' dare you."

"You need to get the fuck off my property, now."

Now he smiled fully, letting me see his too-white teeth. "Look at this guy," he said. "So innocent! But he won't call the cops on a trespasser." He waved a hand at the gravel drive. "I could pitch a tent right here and live on your fuckin' property, and you wouldn't call the cops."

"And you already talked to the cops, and they said you've got jack shit. And you found jack shit in that barn. You're fucking deluded, and if this keeps up *I* will have *you* arrested."

"The cops won't move on it *yet*. It's just a matter of time. It's just that one little piece of physical evidence. Just that one little bit of testimony. They told us to keep at it. The mom, she knows too, and we ain't letting it go. The clock is ticking on you, son. Our friend Isaiah Sever is out there, and once I find that motherfucker all the pieces are gonna fall into place. My advice to you is, fess up first. Go to the cops yourself. You lost your shit? Freaked out and did it? Maybe you cop a plea and it's a manslaughter charge instead of first degree murder. You keep playing it like this? You're doing life, my man. Maximum security with the hard-cases."

"You're fucking crazy," I said. "Get the fuck out of here."

"Now you got the word, son. Now you can stew in it. Kastrel is a wise man. I'm a determined man." He swung a thumb at his overdeveloped chest. "I don't let up. You're gonna wish he was still running this investigation."

We looked at each other for a long two or three seconds. I finally said, "Are you done?"

"Not even close," he said, with a cheesy lift of his eyebrows. And he made a Hollywood exit, turned and dropped off the step and went to his SUV. I stepped back and closed the door before he could give me any more theatrics. I had sweat oozing in my armpits, moistening my forehead. My neck was hot to the touch. I wondered if he had noticed that I was coming apart. I guessed it didn't matter.

I polished the beer and got another. And after that, another. I needed to create a comfortable distance between myself and reality. By the time it was fully dark there were four dead soldiers—as Cliff called empties—on the counter, and reality was over there somewhere; a movie; someone else's ludicrous life. I sat on the kitchen floor in the darkness, forearms on knees, can dangling in my hand, and mulled over my options. I thought for the hundredth time about getting in my truck and just driving away, starting over in a different state, maybe going to Mexico. I had a few hundred in cash, a couple hundred in checking, and twelve hundred and change in the savings account. I felt a tumble inside when I thought of September, and spat a quiet curse, but I knew that she would be better off.

I worked out a little poetry. Falling in love is like an open wound, I thought. What's inside you is exposed. And the wound, over time, slowly becomes part of you, loses its sensitivity, its vulnerability, like a scab forming and then transforming, day by day, into just more of your skin. If you tear the scab off before it knits itself into your existing flesh, there's very little pain. If you wait and pick at it when it's really becoming part of you, it can feel like wounding yourself in a whole new way, and the scar tissue is ugly. Right now, to September, I was a fresh scab. If I waited, if I kept pretending that I was her knight in tarnished armor, and then they got me as they surely would, she would be wounded that much worse. The scar would be a blight that she would have to work to hide. I was drunk enough that that seemed profound.

For about a hundredth of a second, I considered going to the police and confessing. I could admit, I guessed, that I had lost control and done what I had done to Michelle. And Sabrina, well, that was basically self-defense. But what I had to do after—not to the cars, but the other . . . anybody would see that as psychotic. It wasn't, of course. Coroners, forensic doctors, whatever they are, they handle dead human flesh every day. Slice it, saw it, pry at it, stare at it. Then they go home to their families, play with their kids, screw their wives, go to the goddamned Olive Garden and push forks into flesh-colored lasagna and put the rubbery noodles and red sauce right into their mouths. Nobody sees them as sick. I hadn't treated flesh any differently than they do. It wasn't like I had a compulsion. It wasn't like I was happy about it.

I rolled forward, got onto my knees and put Number Five on the counter with the other empties. I opened the fridge and pulled out the last beer, then settled in to get myself to a conclusion. I was buzzed enough that nothing I thought about really stung, really felt personal, but I was not so buzzed that I couldn't do exact math. There was nothing on me unless a search warrant was okayed somewhere and they came here and put every inch of this place under a microscope. They would eventually find the car frames and the other hunks of steel under the dirt in the barn, and they would certainly find the boxes of parts and smashed glass and globs of wires in the attic. They might even find evidence of Michelle and Sabrina. But they wouldn't have to if they found the disassembled cars. I would be caught then, and I would end up confessing.

But—and I realized that this was the proverbial Big But—*but* there would be no search warrant issued unless there was something definite to tie me to the disappearances. And there would be no chance of anyone suspecting me if someone else was tied to the disappearances.

All at once it was so clear that I said, "Holy shit," aloud. Then I said, "Isaiah. Mr. Sever. You stinking goddamn waste of space. You are it. You are my salvation." If inspiration strikes like this, even when you're drunk, it stays with you. It can be something asinine. It can be thinking that you're in love with a twit in a bar or some idea for making a million bucks. You just remember the pillar of light beaming down, the surprise exhilaration, and you think that something outside yourself has communicated with you. I knew that Isaiah Sever could set me free. Mason Smith had explained that to me, after all. Maybe I was just talking myself into what I had already decided must be done. I just had to find Isaiah before Smith did.

21

Good Time Charlie's. Friday night. Nine-thirty. A rap song with electric guitars layered in, blaring at thought-annihilating levels. The panorama in the bar mirror was a hybrid of a good-times beer ad and the cantina scene in *Star Wars*: Girls with their tits all but completely out of their shirts, girls with pierced septums and fluorescent hair, classic sluts with painted-in cheek hollows and sulky expressions, tattooed tough guys, bearded hipsters with 1920s business haircuts . . . I had a plan which was, in retrospect, bizarre. But I had a plan. I told September that a guy I knew asked me to meet him for a beer. I said I would call her when we were done, if she wanted. She said she would be at home, and to call her any time before midnight. All cards on the table. No need to compete, no jealous games, just a girl who knew the whole score and was content to be at home waiting for my call. I was going to earn it. In the fiction I had presented to her, the guy I was meeting was named Jacob. Jacob was a real person, but he had been the boyfriend of Michelle's best friend when I met her, and he was as likely to invite me out for drinks as Donald Trump was.

I had two chances—or more accurately, two desperate hopes. The first, and best, was to walk into Good Time Charlie's and see Isaiah swaying amid the bunches of revelers. From there it would all happen. The second, and far less appealing option, was to talk to Junior, the guy who looked like captain of the high school wrestling team and sold meth, or coke, or heroin, or all that and more. Maybe, then, I would get a lead on Isaiah, and maybe I would find him, if he hadn't already left for California.

I had arrived at nine, and I lingered for an hour, drinking bottles of Bud too fast, before the bottom began to fall out of my confidence. But I should have remembered that Junior had strolled in at maybe eleven, maybe a quarter 'til, two weeks ago. And soon, during my thousandth scan of the barroom, I was looking at that square-jawed, handsome face hovering about five feet and six inches over the barroom floor, talking in a serious—in fact, in a downright businesslike—fashion to four people at one of the raised tables. He had the same just-off-the-barber's-chair fade-cut, and another just-off-the-rack outfit. I breathed all the way in and all the way out a couple of times. My beer was half full. That was good. I didn't want to walk up with a swallow left, trying to swig out of it like a fool because I was too damned wound up and needed to do something with my hands.

I was not ready, but I would do it. I slid off the stool,

strolled around a table, and then I was hovering next to Junior, and he became aware of me and stopped listening to his interlocutors and looked into my face without expression. The people at the table—a black guy, two wanna-Gs, and a female wanna-G wearing a yellow T-shirt borrowed from her five-year-old sister—looked at me with the same empty, questioning hostility.

"You're Junior, right?" All conversations had to be in half-yells.

"Who are you?" he demanded, almost before I had finished my question.

"I'm nobody. Nobody to you. But I need to find a guy you know."

"Not happening," he said, frowning and shaking his head. "I don't know you, dude."

"It's nothing bad," I said. "I have money for him, and I'm trying to help him out."

"Yeah? Who you looking for?"

"Isaiah. I was in here with him a couple of weeks ago and he was talking to you. He said you were cool."

Junior studied me. "Yeah, I remember. You loaned him forty bucks."

"That's right."

"Why you wanna find that fuckin' hobo?" he said.

"I owe him some money. He helped me sell some stuff I had, and I owe him his cut. I don't want to fuck him over."

"Shit," Junior smirked. "*Life* fucked that guy over a long time ago."

The people at the table grinned at that. I grinned along with them.

"Wait over there, dude," Junior said, and indicated the bar with a tilt of his head.

A ripple of indignation rolled through me at being ordered in this way, but there was some kind of jailhouse hierarchy in this place, and I accepted my role as a new fish or whatever the fuck it was. I didn't even make a face in protest. I nodded and said, "Okay. I'll be at the bar. Thanks."

I went to one of the few unoccupied stools and climbed on and worked on my beer. I could see the back of Junior's head in the bar mirror. The song was now an Eminem oldie. *Shady's back. Tell a friend.* After a couple of minutes, Junior tapped my shoulder with the knuckles of his open hand and said, "Aye, buy me a beer and come over here," and walked over to the counter mounted across the big front window, where Isaiah and I had been standing when I'd first seen him. I flagged the bartender, bought two more Buds, and made my way over like an underling hoping to please Little Caesar.

"What the fuck did *Isaiah* help you sell?" he said when I got close.

"Weed. I grew some weed in a barn at my place, and I had . . . more than I could sell legally, so he put me in touch with a guy."

"Who?"

"I don't know his name. He showed up and gave me cash. That's all I know."

Junior nodded, looking out across the barroom. Maybe he thought I was protecting someone's identity and that bought me some respect. He made eye contact and said, "Fuckin' Isaiah's got him an old lady. Like, a real old lady." He smirked. "You know Fortuna?"

"Fortuna? What's that?"

"The fuckin' street."

"Oh, Fortuna Street."

"Yeah, I don't know the number. Big white house. They got a Black Lives Matter sign in the window. He's right there. Up the stairs. Watch out for the fuckin' pits."

"Pits?"

"Fuckin' pit bulls, dude. Jesus Christ."

I had lost focus because Mason Smith was sitting on a bar stool, rotated away from the bar, toward me, staring with unconcealed smugness, his right hand wrapped around a full pint.

"Hey, man," I said to Junior. "Thanks. I really appreciate it."

"No sweat," Junior said. "That fuckin' guy's due for a break. Tell him I said what's up when you give him his scratch."

"I will," I said. "But let me tell you something. There's a great big mulatto dude at the bar, looking over here . . ."

Junior lifted the beer I had bought him, and as he drank his left eye traced down the bar.

"That guy's a cop," I said. "Isaiah brought him around too. I wouldn't talk to him if I was you."

Lowering the beer, Junior said, "Shit. I probably should have shined your ass off. Fuckin' cops following you and shit." He made eye contact with me and said, "Thanks for the beer, guy," and threw his hand so his knuckles tapped my shoulder, and then he was sauntering off, weaving around a table, casually drinking from the beer. He passed Mason Smith without even looking his way, and went to the back of the barroom. Smith looked from Junior to me with a quizzical expression.

The sound system now blared an auto-tuned 'hood-slut musically bitching about being way too good for some dirty dog of a guy. The song would break into double-time rapping periodically, the grating, self-congratulatory voice berating men on fast-forward. It was like being trapped in some ghetto thug's bad acid trip. This whole world suddenly became my personal hell. I put my mostly full beer on the counter beside me and stepped toward the door with my eyes directed straight ahead. Then I was in the cool evening, the bar noise becoming imprisoned as the door closed, my ears now picking up shouting and laughing around a corner somewhere, the nightlife of Holbrook.

I moved down the sidewalk, toward my truck, trying to figure out how I would handle it if Mason Smith followed me out here and confronted me. Then I was in my truck, my cell tossed onto the seat, sliding the machine backward, then clutch, brake, first gear, clutch, second gear, driving drunk in town, having just left a bar, the ideal mark for any lurking cops. I moved the truck like a self-driving vehicle, easy and precise, at the exact speed limit. As I drove I repeated a mantra to myself that went: *A big white house on Fortuna Street with a Black Lives Matter sign in the window. Up the stairs . . .*

At a red light, I picked up my phone and thumbed the button. It was eleven-twenty-five. At eleven-thirty-five I was on a dark road, gliding away from Holbrook, picking up speed. When my right hand was free I thumbed through until I was calling September. Nobody was going to anybody's place this late. Her Christian values. But we started talking in quiet, sleepy tones, and kept talking as I pulled into my drive, and kept talking as I unlocked the house and went inside, and we didn't end the call until after four. As we spoke, I had periodic moments of disorientation, wondering if I had already gone mad. Wondering how I could blink out of the nightmare I was living through and be this other person, this harmless, intelligent guy having a soul-connection with this tragic, extraordinary girl. Wondering if I was actually a hopeless ruin and it was just a matter of time before she and everyone else knew it. At around two a.m., as we talked about what prayers really are, and if they actually work, she confessed that she had been praying for me. "Just to have peace," she said. "Not necessarily, like, the salvation of your immortal soul. There are layers to all this."

You get weird ideas in a dark house, with your whole world a disembodied voice having a conversation with you about unknowable forces and unimaginable entities watching you and taking an interest for some reason in your well-being and your fate for all eternity. I felt convinced for a fleeting moment that God had heard one of her prayers and struck Rod Kastrel down. Maybe Kastrel was happier this way. He was going to be released from the prison of his monstrous body. Maybe he was evil in his own way and paying a debt. Maybe he was the sin of gluttony personified. Maybe there is, like September insisted, a perfect justice that we just don't understand. All the scales balance eventually. It's not even possible to beat the house, so you had better be true in your heart.

I told her to please keep praying for me. It seemed to be doing me some good.

22

When I saw the Black Lives Matter placard in the window of the house I felt a sort of disappointment. I was wishing on some level that I would only turn up dead ends, that fate would conspire against me, and I wouldn't be required, by my misshapen conscience, to follow through with this thing. It was Saturday, just after noon, another ideal spring day with the mercury climbing toward eighty; a day in which, if the world was right, I should be with September somewhere, lost in a love fantasy, picnicking, swimming, doing something dreamy and benign. Instead I was on this street of weed-patch lawns and nuclear test-site houses, trying to connect with a guy who might up and beat the shit out of me at any moment, might pull a gun and shoot me through my intestines, might let his old lady's pit bulls take me down and gnaw off my face.

I rolled by slowly, my head pivoting as I went. The house was a two-story with a front porch and awning so ridiculously off-level that it was like a surrealist painting. The awning was covered in gray asphalt roll-roofing, which was tinged with black rot. What appeared to be an old man, a white-headed blur, was sitting in the shade that the porch afforded. A mismatched staircase was lag-bolted to the side of the house, going to an upper level apartment that had been sectioned off, and I supposed that was what I was looking for. The house had that kind of siding that is all two-inch horizontal strips, tacked on meticulously a hundred years ago by craftsmen who probably worked in dress shirts and had walrus mustaches and eight kids apiece. The durable lead paint of that lost era had finally baked into powder and begun washing away, so bare wood was visible on half the structure, and those old-time Holbrookians, if they could step through a time portal, would stare in utter bafflement at the Black Lives Matter sign divided into neat sections by the multi-paned front window, inevitably missing two of the panes—which was probably the actual purpose of the sign being taped there.

I drove around the block, came back the same way, and parked along the sidewalk, behind a black truck a few years newer than mine that had a truncated bed and a scabbed roll-bar mounted behind the cab. I got out of my truck and death-marched along the crumbling pavement, up the middle of the front yard to the sinking front porch. I nodded to the fat, staring, unkempt old man and followed the crumbling walk around to the side and climbed the sunblasted two-foot-wide staircase that was built of unpainted pressure-treated wood, and felt surprisingly solid. At the top, the door had a funhouse look; an old-fashioned interior door scavenged from somewhere and cut like a randomly cropped photo to match the hole, so there were only thick edges on the right and the bottom. I thought: *building codes lol.* Before I could knock, I heard the rustling and growling of at least two animals. Claws clicking on hard material, throats gurgling like warm-up exercises, percussive barks finally assaulting the air, then ripping out of the canine throats metronomically. It was more effective than any knocker or doorbell, I guessed.

Then I heard his voice. A command to match the dogs' ferocity. "GLENDA! OSWALD! AYE! SHUDDUP! HERE! AYE!" and then a muted thump, and another of the same, and a yelp and whimpering. "Get out the way," Isaiah said. "Siddown. Sit. No. Sit." Then the door knob was shifting, and then a black gap opened and a brass-colored chain pulled taut when the gap expanded to about two inches. Then I was breathing a faint odor of human mixed with dog—with the dog being the less offensive of the two—and looking at Isaiah Sever's sloping, oily face, a single brown eye regarding me, pocked cheeks dotted with lonesome, infrequent hairs, the pubic tangle on his chin.

I waited for him to say something but he just stared. I said, "It's me, Kevin."

"I know who you are," he said. The dogs whimpered their awareness of me, off to his right.

"Junior told me where to find you."

He blinked and released a fetid breath. I leaned back a

little. He made the door knob click, shifting his hand back and forth on it.

"You need to make some money? I got a thing you can do."

"Where are them cops?"

"I don't know. They gave up."

"Don't bullshit me, bro."

"They were trying to set us both up. I haven't seen them since that day at Starbucks."

"Hey!" he said as if I was one of the dogs. "Don't bullshit me."

"I wouldn't," I said. "I've got an easy way for you to make money."

He changed, subtly, at that, and said, "What is it. How much money." There were no question marks on his questions.

"It's, like, acting. I'm in a class, a film class, and I'm making a cheap movie. Fifty bucks just to say some lines. If it works out, you could make a couple hundred bucks just for talking for a few minutes. I need a tough character." My story sounded pathetically transparent when I said it aloud. I had racked my brains but could think of nothing better. I braced for him to tell me to get fucked, to tell me to never show my face here again or else; maybe to open the door and let the dogs have at me.

"Ahh!" he said in a sudden *We know each other well* sound, his cheeks lifting, the space where his front teeth should have been opening up. "You need an Indian. Ain't nobody tougher than a fuckin' Indian. How about seventy-five bucks."

"I don't know about that."

"Come on, bro. Look at you. You got it. I'll go right now for seventy-five."

"You owe me forty, remember?" I said, knowing I was now setting the hook.

His single eye didn't lose its good humor. He said, "Fuck that. I ain't got forty. But you got seventy-five."

"Make it fifty, and I'll forget the forty. That adds up to ninety."

"Ahh!" he said. "You're cheating my ass."

"It's fifty bucks for, like, five minutes of work." Then I thought, *Holy shit, what if he can't read?* But I wasn't going to ask him.

He regarded me for a second, pretending to be unsure. Finally he said, "All right," and gave me a chin-thrust. "Gimme the money. I owe her."

In the dim machinations of his brain he imagined that I knew exactly who *her* was. I said, "I can give you twenty right now. That's all I have in my wallet."

"Do it." His eye blinked a couple of times, drilling at me.

I pulled out my wallet, rotated my body a little, and tilted it toward myself so he couldn't see that I had a few twenties. I extracted the bill and held it out, and his brown hand flecked with white scars shoved out through the gap, clamped onto it, and pulled it inside. "Hold on," he said, and the door closed in my face. There was more ruckus with the dogs, and a brittle female voice in duet with Isaiah's. I could not make out her words but his dead intonations were clear. He said, "My bro. He's making a movie or some shit. Don't worry about it. It's right there. Right fucking there.

Glenda! Oswald! Over there, right now." His voice growled when he addressed the dogs, speaking their language.

Then I heard the chain-latch slide free, the door opened just enough for him to wedge himself out as the dogs made questioning noises, and I stepped down a couple of steps to make room for him on the landing.

We were in my living room, Isaiah's odor a subtle but persistent presence. The blinds were down, but daylight filtered in from the kitchen entryway. I had positioned Isaiah on the recliner that Michelle had picked out. He had one of my tallboys in his hand. On the Big Lots coffee table was my laptop, open and facing him, its battery fully charged.

I said, "The plot is that a female gang is taking over your territory and you just killed the gang's leaders. Have you seen *No Country For Old Men*? Where the old Sheriff gives a monologue? It's like that." I knew that Isaiah didn't care about *No Country For Old Men*, or what my artistic vision might be, but I was attempting to create a sort of haze, to make it less likely that he would recognize any patterns.

He looked at me, unmoving, his mouth partially open. He wore a black T-shirt and jeans, the same broken-down blue and white sneakers he had worn before. On a big folded knee his hand held the tallboy. I was either looking at stupidity itself or he was thinking too hard and this was going to blow up in my face. I had Sabrina's Beretta, safety off, under the striped throw-cushion.

"When I say, 'Action,' just read that one paragraph," I said. "You ready?"

His eyes were slightly glazed. They shifted to the computer screen. He took a swig of beer and then sucked the moisture off his upper lip. He was, I now thought, nervous about his acting ability. I looked at his image reproduced on my phone and said, "Wait. Hold on. Sorry." I turned and reached behind me, rotated the handle and opened the blinds a little. His face had been reflecting the bluish light of the computer screen. Daylight now overpowered the computer glow. "That's way better," I said. "The striped shadows are like classic film noir. Okay, I'm ready. You ready?"

He looked at me, nodded once, and then focused on the computer screen.

I said, "Okay. *Action*," and thumbed the icon.

Isaiah licked his lips and frowned. His head was tilted down to read from the screen but it somehow added authenticity, made him look contemplative. "Ain't nobody ever gonna find them bitches," he said, just slightly better than a first-grader sounding out words. "They're at the bottom of the sea, bro. Them and their fuckin' cars. That shit is over, and I'm running . . . I'm running the show now. They . . . thought they could do man's work. Now they . . . know better." Finishing, he smiled and blinked at me, and said, "Shit, I ain't good at reading, bro. I need to start over."

I said, "No, I think that was perfect. It seemed natural." I had the idea that I could only do one take. I did not know how this iPhone stored filmed material. Was it in a cloud somewhere? What if some expert mined out the history of the device and turned up multiple takes of the same statement? I had stopped the recording just after he looked up. I hoped I had cut off the statement about reading. If not I would have to risk editing it.

I now had to execute the next part of my plan. But I knew all at once that I could not do it. My hand, somehow, would not reach under the cushion. It dawned on me that I didn't know if the gun would shoot, just because the safety was off. Didn't it have to be cocked or something? Hadn't I read in crime books about heroes and villains having to "rack the slide"? I became convinced that if I produced the weapon it would be as impotent as a wooden replica. Then maybe Isaiah would get it from me, and he would know exactly how to use it.

"Lemme see it," Isaiah said.

"Huh?"

"Play it for me. I want to check out my acting, bro."

I stood and thumbed the phone screen, stepping around the coffee table. I opened the video and tapped the arrow as I held the device under his face. I looked at his form, upside down on the screen, plain as anything. His miniaturized voice came out of the speakers: "*Ain't nobody ever gonna find them bitches . . .*"

"Why is your hand shaking so much, bro?" He said.

"Uh, I don't know. My first time directing a movie."

Phone-Isaiah said, " . . . *Them and their fuckin' cars.*"

"Hey," he said, a frown forming, his voice becoming louder. "This could be like a crime confession. You're all sweating and shaking and shit. You could be like . . . "

Before I could decide how to respond, both his hands were closed around my hand and the phone. I brought my other hand into the contest but his grip was like a machine that could increase its pressure indefinitely, until my fingers pinched off along the phone edges. As he got to his feet I was rambling, asking him what the fuck he was doing, and saying, come on, man, what's the matter with you? With his increased leverage he worked his fingers onto the phone, and then hauled backward and ripped it away. My fingers smarted. I shook my left hand at my side and rubbed it with my right.

He said, "This is my phone now, motherfucker," and jammed the device into his back pocket. His nostrils were flared. His face shined. "And you gotta pay me."

"Come on," I said, a childish whine in my voice. "You can't just steal my phone, rob me . . ."

He took a step, brought his right heel back, and field-goal kicked the coffee table so it leapt into the air, as the laptop sitting on its end leapt higher, then bounced off the couch and came to rest sideways, alongside the upended coffee table. "Stop telling me shit, bro! You ain't acting right. Gimme the money or I'm gonna fuckin' take it."

The kicked laptop was what did it. My novel was in its hard drive. No backup. I navigated over the upended coffee table and leaned over the couch as he followed me with his shark glare. I don't know what he imagined I was doing, but he did nothing but watch as I pulled the gun from beneath the cushion and turned back, extending it toward his face. I said, "Take out my phone and toss it on the couch."

For the first time, his gaze seemed utterly lucid. His dead eyes were now soft and alive with fear. His voice even softened, came out as a partial sigh as he said, "All right, bro. I see what it is now. All right." He reached behind him, took out the phone, and tossed it onto the couch.

We looked at each other. The gun was shaking visibly. I bent my arm to my side to keep it steady. He stared at it, rather than into my eyes. I thought that he might recognize it, and he might be putting all the pieces together at this very moment. Then I thought that he might think of his sister, go mad and move for it, and I might squeeze the trigger and get nothing, and then he would kill me with his bare hands, or he would take it and rack the slide and shoot me while I begged. I applied pressure, to test the trigger—

BANG!

My whole head was ringing, the air in the room seeming to shiver in the aftermath. The gun was still in my hand but it had broken loose from my grip. Isiah still stood, unharmed, but shocked. The kick, or my nonexistent aim, had caused the Beretta to fire high. I now brought my left hand over to steady it, and as Isaiah lurched and stretched his arms toward it I fired deliberately, once, before his hands were on it, and again, as his fingers clasped mine and again—as his hands became slack. The second-to-last shot had sent a burst of material like bloody, raw hamburger out of the back of his head. I moved back as he settled on the carpet, face down, next to the upended coffee table.

I had worked it all out. I didn't believe what I was doing as I did it. The shots must come close together. This noise would certainly be noted on a Saturday morning. I jammed the nose of the Beretta into my side, closed my eyes, jerked my index finger in an impulsive fit, and felt the *BANG!* go through me. I was conscious of bits of me being spat out somewhere down behind my left shoulder, but I was confident that I had shredded only flesh, not organs. Then, holding a fistful of T-shirt material at my side, feeling my breath coming short and my system blinking out, I hauled the laptop onto the couch. The screen was half-lost in vertical lines, damaged from its tumble, but the red X at the right corner was accessible and I finger-moused to it and clicked it. Did I want to save the changes to Document 1? No. Microsoft Word closed, leaving the blue haze of the desktop-background only half visible on the broken screen. The fake movie script was gone forever. I closed the laptop, placed it on the floor, and shoved it under the couch. I picked up the gun where I had lain it, and wrapped it in the right side of my shirt, obscuring fingerprints. Then I crawled over to Isaiah's right hand, and wrapped the fat digits around the gun, working carefully, feeling my blood trickling as I concentrated. I took the gun in my hand again, careful not to fire it, and then laid it back on the floor.

I heard myself saying "Ah!" with every breath. I guessed I was a pussy. The shot was not fatal, and I had no other wounds, but spots were appearing in front of my eyes as I picked up my cell, got through the security barrier, and tapped in "9-1-1."

23

A youngish, slightly pudgy sergeant named Rowland interviewed me extensively in my hospital room. I was only there two days, although I still have occasional rips of pain in my side, directly between the small scar in my front and the bigger scar in my back. The police took my phone as evidence. I gave them the security pass and unconditional permission to explore it and I guess they downloaded its full history and contents. I had not taken it with me to the coast, when I smashed Michelle's and Sabrina's cells and dropped them off the pier, into the hypnotic, green-black water. There was no location record, or whatever it was, of my having made that trip. And I generally used the device so seldom that I could not imagine anything incriminating being extracted from it. I was eventually to see the video of Isaiah a hundred times. Once it was released to the public, it was all over the web and finally immortalized in a segment on *Real Killers*, for which I declined to be interviewed.

Each time I watched it, it was agonizingly obvious to me that Isaiah was reading from something, and that was certainly suggested on online discussion boards. One internet genius described the whole scenario, with me as the culprit, with dreadful accuracy, only missing finer details, such as the labor-intensive manner in which I had made the cars disappear (he imagined that I must have deposited them in a body of water somewhere). I read the person's account, which had an almost perfect timeline, had me killing Michelle in a fit of rage, and then killing Sabrina when she came looking, and then luring Isaiah in as a patsy, killing him and giving myself a nonfatal wound after forcing him (at gunpoint in that version) to read the confession. I read all that, feeling myself starting to sweat, and clicked the *X* at the corner of the screen and pretended I had never seen it.

Ultimately, at any rate, Isaiah simply fit the bill too perfectly. It was eventually established that Sabrina had purchased the Beretta at a local sporting goods store, and it seemed quite obvious that the weapon had been in Isaiah's possession from the time that she disappeared.

As I described matters to Rowland, Isaiah had driven Sabrina's car to my house on the night that Sabrina and Michelle disappeared, then a week or two later he had shown up on foot, having taken the bus to the nearby Circle K. He must have disposed of the cars and the bodies sometime between those two events. No, he never gave me any indication of where the cars might be, except for what he said when I filmed him. He had, I said, become convinced that we could manufacture meth in the barn at my house and he was trying to pressure me into agreeing to a *Breaking Bad* business plan. I became convinced, in the meantime, that he had done something to my wife and his sister. When the private detectives began to harass me, especially that Mason Smith asshole, I had decided to fool Isaiah into confessing, and to capture it with my phone. (Yes, I now knew how stupid that was, and I felt like an absolute idiot.) When Isaiah realized that I was filming him, he had pulled out the Beretta and demanded my phone, but as I handed him the phone I grappled with him, and after he fired one shot, which went into my side, I had succeeded in knocking the gun out of his hand, and grabbed it before he could, and shot him several times as he tried to get it back.

Rowland had nodded thoughtfully at my story and said, "I'll be honest with you, Kevin. Only thing that doesn't work for me is, all of this starts with your wife leaving you. To hear this Mason Smith tell it, there's nothing more to any of it than that you lost your temper and killed your wife, and everything else is you covering your tracks. He had a lot to say about an old barn on the property where you live."

"Mason Smith has a one-track mind. My wife was leaving me," I said, "but here's the thing he's ignoring: Isaiah Sever's sister was leaving him. Isaiah was dependent on her. He ended up homeless after she was gone."

I saw Rowland's expression adjust.

I said, "The guy had a tendency to freak out. Mason Smith knows that. Isaiah Sever decked him in the Starbucks. Did he tell you that?"

"I believe he mentioned being punched."

"Isaiah attacked me once, too. I mean, before the last time. I assume he freaked out on Michelle and Sabrina when they told him they were leaving. He probably hated Michelle for taking away the person he relied on for everything. It's not like he was, you know, a gentle type of person or anything."

"You've given this a lot of thought, I see," Rowland said.

"I haven't been able to think about anything else," I said.

Rowland nodded and said it all seemed to add up, he supposed, but he sure hoped they turned up the remains of the girls or at least found the cars. I said I sure hoped they did, too, and that was the last time I talked to the police about any of it.

At Cliff's house, on Thanksgiving, September and I announced that we would be married. Cliff greeted the news with an explosive laugh and a congratulatory slap on my shoulder that nearly knocked me over my plate. He still counted anything other than me being a suicidal shut-in as his own personal accomplishment. Mom, who had no real friction with September but was repulsed, almost physically, by the younger woman's Christianity, drew me aside and told me that I should really think it through, considering the train wreck I had just lived through. Marriage was a-whole-nother thing from just being happy together and she had seen it fuck up too many relationships. I said thanks for letting me in on the secret to your life-success, Mom. She just stared at me, and I just stared back, and she finally said fuck you, Kevin. But she let the topic go.

I only found my faith when I decided to confess to September. I had tried to pray before but I could not take myself seriously. I was excruciatingly conscious of speaking to thin air. But when I knew what I had to do, when I had decided that I would live in a cage, or die of lethal injection, rather than make September's whole existence a lie, I found that God was listening to me, and you may not believe it, but I heard his answer, and after that I was at peace. September and I sat in my living room, and once I began talking I left nothing out—not even the grisly packages, wrapped in black plastic and bound with duct tape, buried only a few moments' walk from where we were as I described them. I told September that I had put the matter in God's hands, and I didn't care about anyone else in this idiotic fucking world, and now that she knew the truth, she was God's agent and she could pray about it, and I would accept whatever I deserved.

That happened on the day before Thanksgiving.

Made in United States
North Haven, CT
20 July 2023

39337882R00124